THE LEAGUE OF
BEASTLY
DREADFULS

HOLLY GRANT

pictures by
JOSIE PORTILLO

THE LEAGUE OF
BEASTLY
DREADFULS

· BOOK 1 ·

Random House New York

Text copyright © 2015 by Holly Grant
Jacket art and interior illustrations copyright © 2015 by Josie Portillo

All rights reserved. Published in the United States by
Random House Children's Books, a division of Random House LLC,
a Penguin Random House Company, New York.

Random House and the colophon are registered trademarks of Random House LLC.

Visit us on the Web! randomhousekids.com

Educators and librarians, for a variety of teaching tools, visit us at
RHTeachersLibrarians.com

Library of Congress Cataloging-in-Publication Data
Grant, Holly.
The league of beastly dreadfuls. book 1 / Holly Grant. — First edition.
pages cm.
Summary: Anastasia, nearly eleven, is snatched from her elementary school
and sent to live at a former insane asylum with two great aunts she had never met
after being told that her parents died in a tragic vacuum cleaner accident.
ISBN 978-0-385-37007-3 (trade) — ISBN 978-0-385-37008-0 (lib. bdg.) —
ISBN 978-0-385-37009-7 (ebook)
[1. Orphans—Fiction. 2. Aunts—Fiction. 3. Kidnapping—Fiction.
4. Shadows—Fiction. 5. Humorous stories.] I. Title.
PZ7.G766757Le 2015 [Fic]—dc23 2013050800

Printed in the United States of America

10 9 8 7 6 5 4 3 2 1

First Edition

for

Muffy
and
Mike

❧❅ CONTENTS ❅❧

THE LEAGUE OF
BEASTLY DREADFULS

1

A Splendid Day for a Funeral

NASTASIA'S DAY BEGAN with a funeral, and it went downhill from there.

Shivering beneath an umbrella, she wondered whether polka-dotted pajamas and fuzzy bunny slippers were suitable funeral attire. The bunnies were perhaps a little too cheerful, goggling at the deceased with bright marble eyes. Well, at least the weather was properly miserable. It was drizzly and dour. The ground squelched with mud, and gray clouds curdled the sky. Anastasia regarded the scraggly November trees with satisfaction, counting seven crows hunched in the bare branches.

Yes, it was a splendid day for a funeral.

Anastasia's father let out a sniffle, and she handed him the tissue box.

"I just can't believe it," Mr. McCrumpet snuffled. "It doesn't make sense. What a tragedy."

"She's going to a better place," Anastasia told him, patting his arm.

"The compost heap?" Mr. McCrumpet cried.

"Well," Anastasia said, "it's a very *nice* compost heap."

They bowed their heads in respectful silence. Rain gurgled in the drainpipes.

"I suppose we should say a few words," Mr. McCrumpet sighed.

"Fred, where's my breakfast?" sounded a nearby bellow. "You know I'm ravenous when I wake up!"

"Coming, dear," Mr. McCrumpet called, his shoulders drooping.

"Dearly beloved," Anastasia said in her best funeral voice, "we are gathered here to say goodbye to our friend Betty Lou."

"Waffles!" screeched the voice from the window. Mr. McCrumpet flinched.

"Betty Lou was a great companion," Anastasia went on.

"What does a woman have to do to get a simple Belgian waffle around here?" Mrs. McCrumpet hollered.

"Betty Lou, we'll miss your hairy lips," Anastasia finished in a rush. "Rest in peace. Is that enough, Dad? I think Mom's about to explode." Besides, her bunny slippers were getting soggy. "Sorry about your plant."

"Another loss." Mr. McCrumpet blew his nose. "And Betty Lou was such a magnificent Venus flytrap specimen. Really first-rate."

"Until she stopped eating flies," Anastasia pointed out.

"Until she stopped eating flies," Mr. McCrumpet echoed gloomily.

"Do you expect the waffles to cook themselves?" came the demand from the window. "And I want my Happy Forest Maple Syrup heated this time! Yesterday it was like eating cold glue!"

"For crumbs' sake, can't a man mourn his Venus flytrap in peace?" Mr. McCrumpet muttered, throwing Betty Lou onto the odiferous jumble of coffee grounds and eggshells before stomping back into the McCrumpet house. Anastasia followed behind, her bunnies squishing with each step.

Mrs. McCrumpet wasn't the only one getting her breakfast late. Anastasia lathered her toast standing up, reflecting that she wouldn't have time to brush her teeth or comb her hair. That was just fine with her. She dunked her spoon back into the marmalade jar, and somehow—this sort of thing was always happening to Anastasia—a glob of orange goop catapulted into her eyes.

"Ouch!" She tottered back from the table.

"Careful!" Mr. McCrumpet looked up from the waffle griddle in alarm. "Look out for Muffy! Don't step on— Uh-oh. Too late."

Everyone knew two things about Muffy, the McCrumpets' pet guinea pig. One: Muffy held a grudge. Two: Muffy was a revenge-pooper. Meaning: Anastasia could expect a nasty surprise in one of her shoes (or perhaps on her pillow) within a day or so.

"Is she okay?" Anastasia gasped, blinking through a haze of orange jam. Mr. McCrumpet was kneeling on the floor, patting the ruffled guinea pig.

"She's offended," he said. "And rightly so!"

A honk outside signaled the school bus was at the curb.

"I'm not even dressed!" Anastasia groaned. "Sorry, Muffster," she apologized over her shoulder as she scrambled to grab whatever was rumpled at the top of the laundry hamper. No time for socks. She was still struggling into her hooded sweatshirt as she burst out the front door and lurched down the porch steps. "Wait! Wait for me!"

Fortunately, the bus paused, its engine chugging.

Unfortunately, Anastasia tripped and fell face-first on the ground.

Fortunately, a squidgy mud puddle cushioned her fall.

Actually, that was pretty unfortunate, too. Dirty water gushed from her nostrils as she twisted around and glared into the smiling plaster face of the garden gnome responsible for her fall. The front yard of the McCrumpet house was, you see, a veritable minefield of garden gnomes. Mrs. McCrumpet liked to order them from the shopping channel on TV.

"Curse you, Winkles!" Anastasia peeled herself off the shabby McCrumpet lawn and limped to the bus. The door wheezed open. "Thanks for waiting, Mr. Butterfield," she panted, pulling her hood over her sopping braids.

The bus driver stared at her for a moment. He stuck his forefinger under the edge of his toupee and scratched his scalp. "Wasn't Halloween yesterday?"

Anastasia rubbed the last bit of marmalade out of her eyes, peering down at yesterday's clothes she had scrounged from the hamper. Oh, *crumbs*! She waved her arms. Fuzzy brown flaps stretched from her sleeves to her side. She felt the seat of her pants and cringed. Yep, the droopy sock she had pinned to her jeans was still there.

It looked like she was going to school as a flying squirrel again.

Slogging to her seat, pretending not to hear the snickers sweeping around the bus, Anastasia reflected that her day couldn't possibly get any worse.

As it happened, she was wrong.

Within forty-two minutes, calamity was to strike Anastasia McCrumpet.

❧ 2 ❧
Premonition of Doom

B Y THIS POINT, you're probably shaking your head and thinking, "My gosh, poor Anastasia McCrumpet! Marmalade in her eyes and teetering on the brink of calamity. And revenge-poo in her future, too. This girl is tragic."

However, Anastasia was not normally prone to calamity or disaster or anything that exciting. She was rather clumsy, I am sorry to say, and often embarrassed herself by falling down or spilling things, but her life was otherwise not marked by mishap. In general, Anastasia's existence was utterly uneventful.

By all outward appearances, Anastasia was a completely average almost-eleven-year-old girl. She had mousy brown hair, mousy brown eyes, and exactly 127 freckles. She dinged a triangle in the school band and always played a tree in

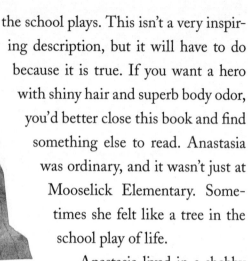

the school plays. This isn't a very inspiring description, but it will have to do because it is true. If you want a hero with shiny hair and superb body odor, you'd better close this book and find something else to read. Anastasia was ordinary, and it wasn't just at Mooselick Elementary. Sometimes she felt like a tree in the school play of life.

Anastasia lived in a shabby little town in a shabby little house with Mr. McCrumpet and Mrs. McCrumpet and Muffy, the guinea pig with anger-management issues whom you have already met. The McCrumpet household also included a variety of plants in various stages of dying. Despite Mr. McCrumpet's best efforts, most of his flora wound up on the compost heap like Betty Lou, the Venus flytrap who went on a fatal hunger strike and whose funeral you have just attended.

Aside from his failures with plants, Mr. McCrumpet had no hobbies or interests. He went quietly about his business selling vacuum cleaners door to door. In fact, he went quietly about everything he did. He even *looked* quiet, if you know what I mean. It was easy to forget he was in the room. His face was like wallpaper.

Mrs. McCrumpet, on the other hand, was *painfully* conspicuous. You couldn't forget she was around, no matter how much you might have liked to do so. She was a big, bloated sea cucumber of a lady, and she was *loud*. She spent all her time clutching a hankie to her forehead and groaning and chugging cough syrup straight from the bottle. There is a kind of person who believes they are sick even when they are not, and Mrs. McCrumpet was just this kind of person. Now, some hypochondriacs are delightful, charming people, but Mrs. McCrumpet was neither delightful nor charming. She was bossy and bad-tempered. She stayed in bed all day long, and when she wanted something, she thumped the floor with the wooden handle of a broom. If that didn't bring Anastasia or her father scurrying upstairs within a couple of seconds, Mrs. McCrumpet started to holler. The longer it took them to come, the louder and pinker she got. By the time Fred McCrumpet hustled upstairs with the waffle tray on the morning calamity befell Anastasia, Mrs. McCrumpet was actually *purple*.

Of course, at that point, none of them had any inkling of the disaster to come.

Anastasia, certainly, wasn't anticipating catastrophe. She had already, I am sorry to say, forgotten about Betty Lou's heartrending funeral. She was scrunched down at her desk, doodling on a sheet of paper crumpled against her knees.

And, if this is to be a thorough account of Anastasia's activities leading up to the moment her fate changed forevermore, I should also mention that she had recently—not even three seconds earlier—*passed gas*. In addition to her mousy brown hair, mousy brown eyes, and exactly 127 freckles, Anastasia McCrumpet also had tragic flatulence.

A few nearby children sniffed the air suspiciously.

Miss Jenkins, the fifth-grade teacher, was droning away by the chalkboard. In her hands she held a thick dictionary, but she wasn't talking about spelling. She was instead telling the students about her pet ferret's stomach problems.

"That's an important life lesson for you, children," she said. "Never feed rice pudding to a lactose-intolerant ferret. Dairy," she intoned, "is the enemy."

A loud knock at the classroom door interrupted this important life lesson. The door had a frosted-glass window, and Anastasia looked up from her sketches to see a shadowy figure lurking on the other side. Something about it gave her the creeps.

Miss Jenkins went over to the door and opened it a little bit and stuck her head out. The students leaned forward in their seats, hoping to catch a snippet of juicy adult conversation, but all they could hear was this:

"Mumble, mumble," muttered the shadow.

"Whisper?" inquired Miss Jenkins.

"Mumble. Mutter, mumble, mumble!" replied the shadow.

"Oh, my goodness. Oh, my gracious! I don't think I've ever heard something so completely appalling in my entire life!" Miss Jenkins cried.

"Mumble, whisper."

All this time, Anastasia stared at that sinister silhouette. She had a terrible sensation in the pit of her stomach that was, for once, not tragic flatulence. No, dear Reader, it was a premonition of doom. (Or, in simple language, a strong feeling that something nasty was about to happen. And boy, was she right.)

"Yes, I'll fetch her right now." Miss Jenkins ducked back into the classroom. "Anastasia? Gather up your things, dear. You're excused from class."

Anastasia crammed her drawing into her book satchel.

"Come along, child," Miss Jenkins prompted.

Anastasia shuffled to the front of the classroom, and then Miss Jenkins hustled her out the door and right into the clutches of the lurking shadow.

"Watch it!" the shadow growled, giving her a shove.

Anastasia stumbled backward, gasping. Then she gazed up into the flaring nostrils of Miss Sneed, the new school secretary. Miss Sneed had only worked at Mooselick Elementary for a few days, but everyone, including the principal, already called her the Monobrow in honor of the long eyebrow bristling across her forehead like a hairy centipede. You will notice I said *eyebrow* (singular) and not *eyebrows* (plural). Most people have two distinct eyebrows, but not Miss Sneed. She had one eyebrow only, and this single eyebrow now snarled into an angry V as she stared down at Anastasia. The classroom door clicked shut behind them. It was the last time Anastasia would ever see Miss Jenkins or, indeed, any of her classmates at Mooselick Elementary. Of course, she didn't know that.

"Follow," the Monobrow barked, turning to stomp down the hall. "Don't loiter. Loitering is for worms."

Anastasia actually *liked* worms, but she nonetheless hurried after the secretary. The Monobrow had shockingly long legs. Her legs were so long, in fact, and she was striding so briskly, that her boot whomped right into the knee of a kindergartner rounding the corner.

"You clumsy cretin!" the Monobrow bellowed. "What are you doing outside your classroom? It is forbidden to walk these hallways without a pass."

"I have one right here," the girl squeaked, holding up a piece of paper.

"Nonsense!" roared the Monobrow, seizing the pass and tearing it in half. She threw the two pieces on the ground. "Pick that up, you filthy litterbug, and get back to your lessons."

The kindergartner danced a little jig. "But I have to go to the bathroom."

"What"—the Monobrow was seething—"is the Mooselick Elementary School motto?"

The kindergartner's mouth hung open. She let out another squeak.

"*Squeak?*" the Monobrow thundered. "Are you telling me the Mooselick Elementary motto is *squeak?*"

"It's *Study Hard and Try to Stay Relatively Clean*," Anastasia whispered.

"That's the old motto," the Monobrow retorted. "The new motto is *Learn to Hold It or Get a Mop*. Commit it to memory, kindergartner. Tattoo it on your arm if you must. Now move it, McCrumpet!" she shouted, clumping onward. "Remember what I said about worms!"

"But Miss Sneed," Anastasia protested, "where are we going?"

"You'll find out soon enough."

Anastasia cast a longing look at the library door as they passed. The library was cramped and dark, but it was still her favorite place in Mooselick Elementary School. It was, in fact, her favorite place in the entire town of Mooselick. The librarian, Miss Apple, often treated the students to mugs of cocoa and homemade cookies. More importantly, she always saved the new Francie Dewdrop mysteries especially for Anastasia. Anastasia admired Francie Dewdrop from the bottom of her heart, and just like Francie, she planned to be a capable detective-veterinarian-artist when she grew up.

Anastasia glimpsed the librarian's pale little face peering out at them over the edge of an enormous book as they marched by. Anastasia raised her freckled hand to wave, but the Monobrow grabbed her elbow and began dragging her down the hall.

"Ouch!" Anastasia yelped.

"Yelping is for worms, McCrumpet!"

The Monobrow hauled her past the cafeteria, past the drinking fountains, past the gymnasium, and all the way to the front door of the school.

"All right, kid," the Monobrow muttered. "Listen here."

Anastasia winced and twisted her face to stare at the enormous hand clinching her arm. The Monobrow's powerful fingers were raw and beefy, and upon her meaty pinkie gleamed a silver ring inscribed with a glowering eyeball. Anastasia marveled at its incredible ugliness for a moment before blinking back up into the Monobrow's face.

"Your parents were in an accident today. They're at Fuzzy Antler Hospital."

"Accident!" Anastasia yawped. "What kind of accident? Are they okay?" Her mind raced with the possibilities.

Mr. McCrumpet had once sprained his ankle on one of the garden gnomes (the dastardly Winkles), and he had broken out in a rash from a pair of polyester trousers one fateful sunny day the previous August. Aside from that, nothing ever happened to Mr. McCrumpet. The very idea that he could wind up in the hospital seemed inconceivably drastic for such a quiet man, to whom nothing interesting had happened in his entire life. And what could happen to Mrs. McCrumpet? She seldom even got out of bed. "What kind of accident?" she asked again.

"Your great-aunts will tell you about it," the Monobrow snapped. "They're waiting outside for you."

Anastasia gaped at her. "But—"

"Behave yourself, McCrumpet," the Monobrow hissed, leaning down so that her mustache tickled Anastasia's ear. "If you dare disobey your aunts, you shall be in a world of trouble. Your buttocks shall be grass and I shall be the lawn mower." On this terrifying note, she bulldozed Anastasia out the front door of Mooselick Elementary.

3

Prim and Prude

TWO TINY OLD ladies huddled on the front steps of Mooselick Elementary, smiling timidly from beneath their enormous umbrella. I'm sure you have seen many old ladies of their ilk. They had rosy cheeks and prune-like faces. Raindrops twinkled on the collars of their bushy fur coats. One of them was a bit stout and had the pushed-in nose of a hedgehog. The other one had twiggy legs and pale pink hair that stuck up in little curls around the brim of her hat.

Anastasia regarded them with begrudging approval. These two old ladies, she thought, looked exactly like two crinkly, stuffy, bespectacled great-aunts should look.

There was just one small problem.

Anastasia didn't have any great-aunts.

"My dear child," warbled the skinny one, "how you've grown!"

"You've sprouted quite a few freckles, I see!" observed the hedgehog.

"Exactly one hundred twenty-seven," Anastasia said. "But I think there's a mix-up. I don't have any aunts." She huffed a sigh of relief. These two old prunes must have come for some other Mooselick Elementary student.

Besides, she thought, wrinkling her nose with distaste,

she wouldn't like to have aunts who went around wearing dead animals. Anastasia, you will remember, was friends with a fluffsome guinea pig. She disapproved of fur coats.

"Why, Anastasia!" the hedgehog said. "We're your Grandpappy McCrumpet's sisters. Bless his heart."

"Rest his soul," added the skinny one.

"Grandpappy?" Anastasia echoed.

The truth was, she had never actually met her grandparents. She had never, for that matter, met any relatives other than Mr. and Mrs. McCrumpet. Her parents didn't talk about them, and they certainly hadn't mentioned any great-aunts.

"Don't you remember us?" the skinny one asked.

"We've *met* before?" Anastasia shivered as rain crept down her neck.

"You were very little," reminisced the hedgehoggy one. "No bigger than a loaf of banana bread. How the time does fly."

"But haven't your parents told you about us?" quavered the skinny one. "They've never said *anything* about Auntie Primrose and Auntie Prudence?"

"Dear me," the hedgehog sniffled. "Oh, my. It breaks an old auntie's heart."

Mortified, Anastasia mumbled, "I guess maybe they mentioned you." But she certainly didn't remember it.

"See, Prude?" the skinny one perked up. "Of course Fred talks about us!"

"Such a dear boy," Prude said. "Prim, remember how he visited us every summer? How he loved to vacuum the hall rugs!"

A fellow named Fred who loved to vacuum? That was Mr. McCrumpet, all right.

"Now, why exactly is there a tail dangling from your trousers?" Prim asked. "Are you dressed up as—as a *wolf*?"

"No." Crimsoning, Anastasia flapped her arms to display her wings. "I'm a flying squirrel."

"Thank heavens," Prim said. "Wolves are so very scary."

"They eat little old ladies and small children, you know," Prude said, clutching at her chest.

"Um," Anastasia said. "The Monobrow—I mean, Miss Sneed—said Mom and Dad are in the hospital. What happened to them?"

The aunties exchanged a fretful look. Prude unsnapped her purse and rummaged around for a minute before pulling out a linty conglomerate of ancient peppermints. "Have a sweetie," the old lady said. "It always helps to have a sweetie before bad news."

"No thanks," Anastasia said hastily.

"Just a lick," Prude persisted, shoving the lump forth.

"Really," Anastasia said, "I'm not hungry."

"One little lick!" urged Prude. "Yum, yum!"

"A spoonful of sugar helps the medicine go down," Prim encouraged her.

Anastasia looked at the two flustered old ladies, and she squinched her eyes shut and stuck out her tongue.

"Delicious, isn't it?" Prude crammed the disgusting glob back into her handbag. "My favorite candy, and so economical. Why, that one piece has lasted me over two whole years! I'm sure I've licked it thousands of times."

"Well," said Prim, "we really ought to get going."

"But you still haven't told me what happened to Mom and Dad!" Anastasia exclaimed. "Are they okay?"

"We'll tell you on the way," said Prude. "If we stay out in this rain much longer, we'll catch pneumonia!"

"But—"

A thunderclap drowned out Anastasia's protest. The aunties went scurrying down the steps of Mooselick Elementary, screeching "Ooooh! Ooooh! *Ooooh!*" as their sensible shoes splashed through the rainbow-streaked puddles of the parking lot. Anastasia raced after them to a station wagon painted an astonishing shade of pink.

"In you go, dear," Prim said, flinging the back door open. "And *do* try not to get mud on the upholstery."

The station wagon was already squealing away from Mooselick Elementary and down the rain-slicked road when Anastasia noticed the cage.

The front seat was separated from the back of the station wagon by a panel of wire mesh. Anastasia reached forth and crooked her index finger through one of the metal loops. "What's this?"

Prim swiveled slightly. "This station wagon used to be owned by a dog groomer," she said.

"We got a marvelous deal on it," Prude said. "You must never buy a new car, Anastasia. It loses half its value the second you drive off the lot."

"But why is there a *cage*?" Anastasia asked.

"It was to prevent the pooches from jumping into Claude's lap or nibbling his ears," Prim explained.

"Claude?"

"The dog groomer!"

They whizzed down the highway. Anastasia twisted the ends of her braids, watching raindrops squiggle down the window like glass worms. Then she spotted a big sign on the side of the road that said THANK YOU FOR VISITING MOOSELICK in tall orange letters.

"Hey!" she shouted. "You missed the turn to Fuzzy Antler! We have to go back!"

"Fuzzy Antler?" Prim asked, staring back at Anastasia.

"The hospital!" Anastasia said. "Miss Sneed said Mom and Dad are at Fuzzy Antler Hospital!"

"Oh." Prim's fluffy head wobbled a bit. "Well, Miss Sneed was mistaken, dear. Your parents are at St. Shirley's Hospital for the Seriously Mangled, which is several hours away."

"They airlifted them in a helicopter!" piped up Prude. "Isn't that fancy?"

"*Seriously mangled!*" Anastasia spluttered.

"Now, now," said Prim. "They'll be fine. It was just a freak vacuum-cleaning accident. And Dr. Mantooth at St. Shirley's is supposed to be the best surgeon in the country for that sort of thing."

"My parents are having *surgery*?"

"Sitting like this is putting a knot in my neck," Prim said. "My poor old bones can't take it." She turned her back to Anastasia.

"But, Aunties!" Anastasia jingled the partition.

"You're tarnishing the mesh, dearie," called Prude, eyeing Anastasia in the rearview mirror. "Kindly remove your sticky hands."

Anastasia slouched back, worry curdling her stomach. She wondered whether her dad had accidentally vacuumed off Mrs. McCrumpet's toes while tidying up the specks of waffle crumbs that always littered her bedsheets after breakfast. It was a gruesome possibility.

Struggling to shake away these terrible thoughts, she began to tally the cars plastered with interesting bumper stickers. LABRADOODLE ON BOARD. The station wagon's heater blasted away, gusting Anastasia's wet clothes. HONK IF YOU HATE LOUD NOISES. Her eyelids drooped, and she must have dozed off sometime after I BRAKE FOR MOOSE DOO, because the next thing she knew it was dark outside, her bottom was numb, and her teeth felt mossy. The backseat was muggier than a Florida swamp. Anastasia used the side of her fist to rub away a little circle of the steam silvering the window and peered out into the rain. The station wagon bumped along a road twisting between steep hills.

"Where are we?" she croaked.

"Look who's awake! Did you have a nice nap, dearie?" Prim asked. She was clicking away with two extra-long knitting needles, crafting something pink and lumpy.

The sky growled, and a terrific flash of lightning dazzled the murk. For just a second, Anastasia could see the road snaking through the forest, zigzagging all the way to a huge castle humped at the tippity-top of the tallest hill. Dozens of towers spiked its roof, biting into the clouds. Then darkness swallowed up the sinister view.

Anastasia blinked, seeing the jagged outline of the castle on the insides of her eyelids. "Is *that* the hospital?"

"No, my dear," Prim replied. "That's where we'll be spending the night."

"In that castle?" Anastasia's jaw dropped.

"Castle! Did you hear that, Prude?" Prim chuckled. "It isn't a castle, Anastasia. It's just a very big house."

"A historical Victorian mansion!" Prude added.

"But why are we spending the night *there*?"

"The storm is getting worse. We can't drive all the way to St. Shirley's tonight," Prim said.

"But what about Mom and Dad?"

"The nurse telephoned and said they're on the mend,"

Prim replied. "But they need to rest. We'll visit them tomorrow."

Anastasia frowned. "When did the nurse call?"

"You were napping," Prude said. "We didn't want to wake you."

The station wagon juddered as they rounded another harrowing curve, and then chugged to a stop. The headlights carved a silver tunnel of light through the gloom, and at the end of this tunnel gleamed the warped bars of an old iron fence. Anastasia squinted to read the crooked sign hanging from one of the bars:

SAINT AGONY'S ASYLUM
for the
DERANGED, DESPOTIC, DEMENTED
&
OTHERWISE UNDESIRABLE
(THAT IS TO SAY, CRIMINALLY INSANE)

❈ 4 ❈
Fingernails on Glass

LIGHTNING SHREDDED THE sky, illuminating the ghoulish mansion crouching behind the fence. Anastasia knotted her fingers through the cage. "Hey! *Hey!*"

But Prim went on knitting, and Prude pressed a button on a little remote control clipped to the driver's-side visor. The gates swung open, and the pink station wagon crawled through the mud toward the fortress.

Anastasia sat back, hugging her satchel. Why on earth were they spending the night at St. Agony's Asylum for the Deranged, Despotic, Demented, and Otherwise Undesirable (That Is to Say, Criminally Insane)? She twisted around and watched as the electric gates clanked shut behind them. How had they wound up *here*, on top of a hill in the middle of a forest in the middle of nowhere? How many thugs lived in that creepy place? What sort of crimes had they committed?

Thunder rumbled, and the sky went dark. The wagon groaned and stalled.

"Oh, poo," said Prude. "We're stuck." She revved the engine. It sputtered, but the car did not move. Anastasia squeezed her satchel even tighter.

And then she heard the noises.

It first sounded a little bit like mice squeaking at her window. Anastasia strained her eardrums. Not *quite* mice. The noise was like teeth grinding together. Or . . . like something scraping the glass.

Fingernails.

"Aunties!"

The clouds flared with lightning again, and Anastasia saw what was making the noises: two white hands clawing the glass, the fingers long and curled. Anastasia's heart thumped three times before clouds gulped the lightning and gloom curtained the window.

It was probably only a few seconds before the next flashbulb of lightning, but it seemed an eternity, perhaps because it is very unpleasant to sit in the dark and listen to screams of terror. Surprisingly, Anastasia wasn't the one screaming. She was too frightened even to peep.

The screams weren't coming from the front seat, either. They were coming from *outside*, Anastasia realized, when the next burst of lightning blazed like a spotlight on the awful scene beyond her window. Prim was out in the rain, walloping away with the pointy silver end of her umbrella. "Get away, you filthy beast!" she shrieked. "Away, you dreadful creature!"

The target of these fearsome brollie wallops was a scrawny teenaged boy, his head hidden inside some sort of odd birdcage. A bell fastened to the cage tinkled hysterically as the umbrella crashed down. *Tingalingalingaling!* Anastasia caught a glimpse of wild eyes before his palms squealed from the glass and he tumbled backward into the mud, howling.

"Shoo! Shoo, I say!" The umbrella clobbered the cage. *TINGALINGALING!*

"Get away!" Prim jabbed the ruffian's ribs with her umbrella. He yowled and staggered off into the fog.

Prim unfurled the umbrella and opened Anastasia's door. "We're here!" she announced with a bright smile.

Anastasia gawped at her. "We're actually staying here? In this insane asylum?"

Prim giggled. "No wonder you look so frightened!" she said. "This *used* to be a lunatic asylum, but that was over one hundred years ago. Now it's just a big old house, like we told you. A very pretty one, too," she added, beaming at the sinister mansion.

Anastasia gulped. "Is this *your* house?"

"Indeed it is," Prim replied proudly. "We got it at a fantastic price. For some reason, nobody wanted to buy a historic lunatic asylum."

Anastasia could think of about twenty terrific reasons right off the top of her noggin, but she didn't utter them out loud.

"Out of the car, dearie," Prude said, joining Prim under the umbrella.

"But who was that boy you just attacked?"

"I wasn't *attacking* him!" Prim twittered. "That was the Gardener. And he knows full well that he's supposed to stay out of this rain. He gets the sniffles."

"Delicate lungs," added Prude. "But you know how teenagers are. So willful! Always refusing to wear a coat in chilly weather."

"But why did you *hit* him?" Anastasia persisted.

"Because, my dear," Prim said, "youngsters should mind nice little old ladies. It's manners. And now I would like you to follow us."

Anastasia hopped out into the downpour and trod miserably behind her aunties. "Why is your Gardener wearing an old birdcage on his head?"

"It isn't just any old birdcage," Prim said. "It's an elegant Victorian antique. And it's a precaution against certain—er—hazards."

"Biting," Prude said.

"Yes," Prim said. "Quite an accomplished biter, the Gardener."

"He's a bit mad," Prude said.

"A bit!" Prim cried. "He's a complete lunatic!"

"You may have noticed that our lunatic Gardener has a bell attached to his birdcage," Prude said. "That's to warn you of his approach. Best to scurry off to safety if you hear bells in this house."

"Yes," Prim said. "Don't go thinking it's an ice cream truck."

"Ice cream trucks," Prude said sadly, "never venture into these woods."

"But why would you hire an insane Gardener?" Anastasia demanded, dragging her feet up the front steps.

"Do you know how much *sane* gardeners charge these days?" Prude exclaimed. "It's outrageous! We can barely afford our biting loony!" She pushed her spectacles to the tip of her nose and peered at an enormous brass dial bulging, like an outie belly button, from the center of the door. She tweaked the nub, and it hiccuped *click click click click click*.

"I've never seen a combination lock on a door," Anastasia said.

"Well, I imagine you've never seen the front door of a former asylum for the criminally insane," Prim said. "The locks and bolts of St. Agony's are the crème de la crème.

Designed by a brilliant master locksmith, they were. Had to withstand the efforts of baddie safecrackers and lock pickers, you understand."

Prude gave the disk a final twirl and the door swung open. "Mind the mirror," she cautioned, her shoes squeaking on a silver-framed mirror bolted across the stone stoop. "It's slick."

"Why do you have a mirror on your porch?" Anastasia asked.

"My goodness, you're a curious girl! It's just part of the authentic Victorian decor." Prim rattled the raindrops from her umbrella and wrestled it shut. "Come along."

They bumped around in the dark. A match flared.

"Here's your candle, dearie." Prude shoved forth a candlestick, a bulbous ring flashing on her pinkie. Something quivered deep in Anastasia's belly.

"The school secretary has that ring, too," she said.

"Oh, really?" Prude said. "I ordered it off the shopping channel on television. Fetching, isn't it?"

Anastasia accepted the heavy candlestick and brandished it through the gloom. Furniture draped with sheets loomed around them.

"This is the Great Hall," Prude said, matches sizzling between her fingertips as she lit the tapers of a tarnished candelabrum. "Isn't it beautiful? Think of all the Victorian criminals who gallivanted beneath these historic ceilings!"

Gawking upward, Anastasia could just make out the shadowy shapes of chandeliers cocooned in cobwebs.

"This way, child." The candelabrum's glow bobbled deeper into the asylum.

"Why are we using candles?" Anastasia asked. "Did the storm knock out the power?"

"We're using candles," Prude replied, "because St. Agony's doesn't have electricity."

"It's more authentic that way!" declared Prim.

"Authentically *what*?" Anastasia mumbled, eyeballing the cobwebby head of some dead furry thing bolted to the wall. "Authentically creepy?"

"There's only one thing that runs on electricity here," Prude said, "and that's the fence that goes all around the estate."

"Buzzing with ten thousand volts," Prim said. "If you touched it, you'd frizzle to a crisp!"

"A crisp?" Anastasia gasped. "But why— Ouch!"

BRZZZING!

"Careful!" Prim called. "Mind the harpsichord!"

The aunties veered toward a burly wooden banister and began the long climb upstairs. Anastasia gazed up the stairwell. A pink-patterned carpet runner spooled down the steps like a monstrous spotty tongue.

"Come along, moppet!" Prim coaxed.

A row of portraits lined the green wall, their canvases

so caked with dust that Anastasia could barely detect the ghostly outlines of painted figures. Her skin prickled as she tiptoed past this sinister gallery and up to her aunties.

"Whew," Prude wheezed at the top step. "I have to rest a minute." She plonked her candelabrum on the newel post and pulled a plastic bottle out of her pocket. She shook two tiny white tablets onto her palm. "Heart medicine," she panted.

"Oh, what frail old ladies are we," Prim lamented, leaning on the handle of her umbrella as though it were a cane. "Anastasia, don't be surprised if your auntie Prude and I don't even make it through the night."

"Little old ladies often die in the middle of the night, you know," Prude added.

Anastasia was horrified. What if she found her aunties dead the next morning, lying stiff on the dusty floor like two little hamsters someone had forgotten to feed?

"Yes," Prude said, scarfing the tablets and pocketing the bottle. "The life of a little old lady is precarious indeed. Death lurking around every corner."

They started down a hallway so long that Anastasia would have needed a telescope to glimpse its end. They walked past door after door after door. Each door had a little metal number screwed onto it, and Anastasia announced the numbers as they passed. "Twenty-nine . . . twenty-eight . . .

twenty-seven . . . ," she counted. ". . . fifteen . . . fourteen . . . twelve . . . Hey!" she exclaimed. "What happened to thirteen?"

"Lots of old places don't have a thirteenth room." Prim shrugged. "Superstition. Unlucky thirteen, you know."

"Here we are, number eleven!" Prude said. She pulled an enormous key ring from her purse. "This is where you'll sleep tonight, Anastasia. You lucky little girl! What fun! It will be just like staying in a hotel!"

Anastasia stared doubtfully at the chain looped from the jamb to the edge of the door. "Really?"

"Oh, yes," Prim chirped. "In fact, we think St. Agony's would make a delightful bed-and-breakfast! So quaint! So charming!"

"So *authentic*," Anastasia added, looking down at the mirror gleaming on the carpet like a bizarre welcome mat.

The lock clunked, and Prude slid aside the chain. "Now be a Nice Little Girl and scoot right to bed," she said. "And don't be scared by any noises you might hear."

"Noises?" Anastasia echoed.

"You know," Prude said, "creaking or footsteps. This is a very old house, and sometimes old houses make funny noises."

"Sometimes, the house makes a cute noise kind of like a man screaming in anguish," Prim said cheerfully. "But it's just St. Agony's, settling into its foundations!"

"After a while, you get used to it," Prude said. "Yes, it gets to where you *like* what perhaps sounds like fingernails scratching at a locked door but is really just an old building groaning."

"And rasping," added Prim.

"And squealing. But," Prude went on, "you probably won't hear a thing. These walls are nice and thick, and Room Eleven is cozy as can be. You'll be snug as a bug in a rug once you're locked—"

"Tucked," Prim said quickly.

"Yes, yes, I meant *tucked* inside."

The two old ladies beamed at her. Anastasia's gaze yo-yoed between their sweet faces. "But," she said, and hesitated. There were so many *but*s, she couldn't decide which one to bring up first.

"No buts," Prim said. "It's bedtime for Nice Little Girls."

Anastasia planted her feet in the doorway, loath to go into the dark room. "But what about my good-night story?" she asked. "And I don't have pajamas."

"Now, now, no more excuses," said Prude. "Beddy-bye time, young lady."

"But I don't have a toothbrush," Anastasia stalled.

"That's all right," said Prim. "Neither have we. And our teeth are just fine, aren't they, Prude?"

Both little old ladies grinned at her, curling their lips up from their pale pink gums and showing their teeth for the first time that day. Anastasia gasped and took a step backward. She was so shocked by the aunties' teeth that she actually took *two* steps backward, right into Room Eleven.

"Sweet dreams," whispered Prim, before the door slammed shut and the key moaned in the lock.

❧ 5 ❧

The Child-Shaped Hollow

THE METAL CHAIN clattered through its track on the other side, and Anastasia leapt forward to grab the knob. She tried to twist it, but it didn't budge.

Reader, there are greeting cards for many occasions. There are cards for birthdays. There are Hanukkah and Christmas cards, and soppy pink Valentines trimmed in lace, and "Get Well Soon" cards. There are even "Thank You for Pet-Sitting" cards. However, as of the printing of this book, no card manufacturer has ever marketed a "Congratulations on Your Very First Premonition of Doom!" card. Nor can you easily find a "Sorry You're Frightened out of Your Gourd Because You're Locked in a Former Lunatic Asylum in the Middle of Nowhere on the Day Your Parents Were Mangled in a Freak Vacuuming Accident" card. It's a shame, because a card like one of these would have been perfect for Anastasia at this dreary point in our story.

Holding her breath, she pirouetted to face Room Eleven. A narrow cot on a spindly metal frame cowered against one wall. The mattress, quilted in cobwebs and dust, sagged in the middle where someone—someone about Anastasia's size—had once lain. Anastasia could even make out the faint impression of a head and arms and legs. It reminded her of snow angels, but in a creepy way.

A behemoth wardrobe hulked against one wall, grim and sturdy as the Monobrow. Anastasia tiptoed closer and bravely flung the doors open. She heaved a sigh of relief. The only thing lurking in the wardrobe was a bunch of musty fur coats, just like the ones Prim and Prude had been wearing all day.

EeeeeeOOOOOO!

Anastasia leapt straight into the air, her candlestick crashing to the floor. What in blue blazes was *that*?

EeeeoooooOOOO!

Goose bumps sprang up over Anastasia's freckled epidermis. Was it someone crying? It didn't sound *human*. It sounded, actually, rather like the whale calls Miss Apple had played for the fifth graders at Mooselick Elementary during their library unit on marine biology. Miss Apple was a real science enthusiast.

OOOooooooooo . . . ooo. The wails grew softer and softer until they faded away completely. It must have been,

Anastasia thought, the wind wuthering at the walls of St. Agony's Asylum. But her legs wobbled as she stood up.

She retrieved her candlestick and shoved the coats to one side, revealing a gray lump cuddled in the wardrobe's dark belly. She stooped to pull it out.

"A stuffed bunny?"

She slowly turned it over, squishing the sagging cloth body between her fingers. Had, one hundred years earlier, a criminally insane child imprisoned the bunny in the wardrobe? The rabbit's dirty tail clung to its knit bottom by a single thread, and one of its button eyes was missing. Anastasia thought with a pang of her bunny slippers at home, kicked aside in the scramble to get dressed for school that morning. She wondered whether Muffy had revenge-pooped in one of them or, perhaps, in both.

"Well, Mr. Bunster, it looks like we're roommates for the night," Anastasia informed the rabbit, plopping him down on the forlorn mattress. Her tummy mumbled, and she realized she hadn't eaten since her disastrous breakfast hours earlier. She hunkered on the floor and dug her peanut butter sandwich out of her satchel. It was mashed after all the excitement of the day, but Anastasia was too hungry to care. She gobbled it down in three bites, and then rummaged through the trick-or-treating booty jumbling her tote. Dozens of sour watermelon taffy nuggets rustled

amongst candy bar wrappers, but for reasons we shall discuss later in this story, Anastasia had sworn off sour watermelon taffy for life.

Why hadn't her aunties given her dinner? Or at least a bedtime snack? And why, for that matter, had they locked her into a spooky room? So far, Anastasia was not exactly thrilled with Primrose and Prudence. No wonder her parents had never mentioned them. Mr. McCrumpet was probably happy to pretend they didn't exist.

Besides, anybody would be glad to forget those awful teeth.

Anastasia shivered. Why did Prim and Prude have *metal* teeth? Were they some kind of weird dentures? They looked so *sharp.*

"The better to eat you with, my dear," she muttered to Mr. Bunster.

The candle had burned down to a stump. It would soon fizzle out. Anastasia decided to inspect the one remaining pocket of gloom in Room Eleven while she still had a smidgen of candlelight—just in case.

"If you don't mind," she told the stuffed rabbit, "I'm going to check under the bed." She peeked below the rusted springs. Candlelight glinted off something squatting against the baseboard, and Anastasia stretched her arm into the darkness. Dust twitched her nose into a colossal sneeze. Her fingers closed around a porcelain handle, and with quite a ruckus of clinking and clunking, she dragged forth what proved to be a whopping great teacup.

She blinked at it. The cup was *enormous*. Who in the world would use such a huge mug? It was just the right size for an elephant tea party. Actually, Anastasia mused, it looked rather like a—

"Chamber pot!"

Chamber pots, in case you don't know, are big bowls used as toilets in places that do not enjoy the luxury of modern plumbing. Anastasia had seen a chamber pot at the Mooselick Museum of Plumbing and had quivered at the grim idea of ever hovering over one and trying to do as nature intended. "How authentic," she grumbled.

It was a fitting end to a perfectly poopy day.

"Anastasia! Nice Little Girls sit up straight at the breakfast table!"

Anastasia slouched valiantly against her hard wooden chair. She didn't care one whit about being a Nice Little Girl. She had spent a terrible night trembling in the child-shaped hollow of the rotten mattress in Room Eleven. She had woken with a cobweb gumming up her left nostril.

And she had, despite all her heroic efforts to the contrary, *actually used the chamber pot.*

She tried to put this horror out of her mind as she prodded the colorless glop in her bowl. "What is this, exactly?"

"Mystery Lumps," chirped Prim. "Isn't that fun?"

"Fun?" Anastasia echoed.

"Everyone enjoys a good mystery!" Prude said.

Anastasia lifted her spoon to her nose and sniffed. "It smells," she mused, "like wet socks."

"Anastasia!" Prim looked scandalized.

"I'm trying to solve the mystery!" Anastasia tilted her spoon, watching the Mystery Lump slither back into her bowl.

Although it smelled like wet socks, her breakfast wasn't even the creepiest element in the dining room at St. Agony's Asylum. That distinction went to the shabby animal trophies mounted high on the moldy walls. Anastasia wrinkled her nose. "Don't you feel weird with all these decapitated heads watching you eat?"

"Not at all," Prude said. "They're adorable! We've even named our little menagerie. That one," she said, pointing at a wolf glowering overhead, "is Beauregard."

"Prude named it that," Prim said. "After the wooer in one of her romance novels."

Prude's face turned pink. "Anyway, Anastasia," she said, "don't you like animals?"

"I love animals," Anastasia said. "That's why I *don't* like this dining room."

Prude narrowed her eyes. "This is a fine old room. Think of all the people who dined at this table before us, enjoying their puddings and plum puffs."

"The authentic Victorian history!" Prim rhapsodized. "Did you know, Anastasia, that the inmates of this asylum dressed for dinner every night?"

"They wore tuxedos with tails and evening dresses and gloves up to their armpits," sighed Prude. "I've seen photographs. There was one particularly handsome arsonist. Sideburns to rival those of a gorilla. Rather dashing."

"Barmy and criminal they may have been, but they had good table manners," Prim declared. "Now sit up straight and eat your Lumps."

Anastasia fell silent, shivering. The dining room at St. Agony's Asylum was as cold and clammy as an octopus hug. It was so cold, in fact, that her aunties were wearing their fur coats, dragging their furry sleeves through their repulsive breakfasts. Chill seeped into the worn soles of Anastasia's sneakers.

She shivered even harder. "I heard a strange noise last night, Aunties."

"Oh, really?" Prim said, stirring her tea. "And what is it, exactly, that you think you heard?"

"It sounded like this." Anastasia rounded her mouth and let out her most mournful "*Ooooooooooo.*"

"Don't do that!" Prude cried. "You sound like a wolf!"

"We told you not to mind any peculiar noises you might hear," Prim said. "I'm sure it was just the wind. Can't you hear it coming down the chimneys?"

"Or perhaps you heard our poodles howling," Prude suggested. "They go absolutely wild if their dinner is even five minutes late. The poor dears were famished by the time we got home last night."

"You have poodles?" Anastasia squinched her eyes to peer through the rain blurring the window. Fuzzy animal shapes galloped amongst the enormous bushes clustering the field of mud. Beyond this morass jutted the iron fence, and behind the fence loomed a forest of spiked trees.

Prude also looked out the window. "The Dread Woods," she said slowly.

"Not a nice place," Prim whispered.

"We don't go there," Prude said.

"Why not?" Anastasia asked.

Her aunties exchanged a nervous look. Then Prude said, "Please pass the pickles, Prim."

Mystery Lumps was the main dish on the breakfast table, but there was also a jar of pickles floating in yellow-green brine. Anastasia watched as Prude fished one out. *CHOMP! CLANK! CLUNK!*

"Why are your teeth like that?" Anastasia blurted.

Prude swallowed. "Like what?" She delicately licked the brine from her fingertips.

"Metal," Anastasia said.

"So you've noticed our teeth," Prim said. "Well, dear, as you get older you'll lose your teeth, too."

"We couldn't afford nice pearly dentures," Prude sniffled.

"Certainly not after purchasing this asylum fitted with fanciful locks," Prim said.

They both looked so dejected that Anastasia felt guilty for bringing it up. She quickly changed the subject. "Speaking of locks," she said, "why did you lock me into my room last night?"

"Safety," Prim said. "We didn't want you to go wandering, dear. This is an old and unpredictable house."

"You could fall through a weak floorboard and break your leg, or step on a nail and perish from lockjaw," Prude said. "That's why most of the asylum is completely sealed off."

"And the basement," Prim added, "is absolutely forbidden."

"And *do* promise us you won't venture into the North Wing," Prude said. "It's also off-limits. Very cold, you understand. You could get frostbite!"

"Don't worry," Anastasia said. "I'm not going to wander off before we leave. How far is it to the hospital? Will we be there before lunch?"

"Your parents need to rest, dear," Prude replied. "Now yummy up those Lumps."

"And then perhaps we'll go outside to play," Prim said. "Won't that be nice?"

"But what about Mom and Dad?" Anastasia said. "You still haven't told me exactly what happened to them."

"Not a very pleasant subject for the breakfast table," Prim said.

"Maybe we'll discuss it tomorrow," Prude said.

"Tomorrow!" Anastasia said. "Aren't we going to St. Shirley's today?"

"Oh, I don't think so," Prude said. "Maybe on Thursday."

"Or Friday," Prim said.

"Friday!" Anastasia exclaimed. "We might be here until Friday?"

"Anastasia, finish your Mystery Lumps," Prude said. "You can't have a good day if you don't eat a good breakfast."

"But this *isn't* a good breakfast!" Anastasia cried. "And I'm not going to have a good day, anyway! My parents are in the *hospital*, for crumbs' sake!"

Her aunties stared at her in stunned silence. Then Prim dabbed at the corners of her mouth with her napkin. "My dear child," she said. "We were trying to spare your feelings."

"Yes," Prude said. "We wanted to find the best way to break it to you."

"Break what to me?" Anastasia asked.

"The bad news," Prude said.

"Awful news," Prim quavered. "Just awful."

"What news?" Panic clotted Anastasia's throat. "What are you talking about?"

"Oh, dear," Prude fretted. She reached under the table and picked up her purse and unclasped the top. "Peppermint? A spoonful of sugar—"

"Just tell me whatever it is you have to say!" Anastasia bellowed.

The peppermint lump fell out of Prude's hand and thudded to the floor.

"Anastasia," Prim murmured, "your mommy and daddy are dead."

❦ 6 ❧
The Silver Heart

YOU NEVER KNOW how you will react to shocking bad news until you get it. Some people gasp "Oh!" and faint. Some people scream and tear at their hair. And some people go completely quiet. Anastasia belonged to this last category. She opened her mouth, but no words came out.

"They took a turn for the worse around midnight," Prude said. "The hospital sent us a telegram this morning. Sorry, dear."

"Dead?" Anastasia finally managed to whisper.

"Dead as dormice," Prude said sadly.

"Doornails," Prim corrected her. "Doornails, Prude. Dead as doornails."

"That doesn't make sense," Prude said. "Doornails are

never alive to begin with, so how can they be dead? Now, two sweet little dead dormice are *terribly* poignant."

"But that isn't the expression," Prim protested. "Besides, dormice are so sleepy, I daresay they're practically half-dead their whole lives."

"I had a pet dormouse once," Prude said. "And she was very lively."

"Nonsense!" Prim said. "That mouse wasn't your pet. You caught it to feed to Margot."

"Ah, yes," Prude agreed. "My beloved boa constrictor. My, how that silly mouse jumped! Which proves my point. Extremely energetic, that mouse."

"She was trying to escape Margot," Prim pointed out.

"Well," Prude said with a smile, "she didn't." She glanced over at Anastasia, and the pleasure faded from her round face. "Your parents," she sighed, "are dead as something very dead indeed."

"So sad," Prim said. "You're an orphan now, of course."

"Oh, my." Prude shook her head. "An orphan. Now, that is tragic. Motherless, fatherless . . ."

"All alone in the world," Prim piped up.

Anastasia had read about orphans in storybooks. To an almost-eleven-year-old girl with two parents, orphans had been sort of a mythical figure, like unicorns and mermaids. A creature that lived in the pages of a book. And now she was one. An orphan, that is. Not a unicorn. She shook her head, feeling dizzy. Perhaps she would faint, after all.

"Oh, my poor child!" said Prim. "Don't worry! There's a silver lining to this woeful storm cloud."

"That's right," Prude chimed in. "Very happy news!"

Can you guess, Reader, what splendid announcement Anastasia's great-aunties had tucked up their furry sleeves? I can imagine very few revelations that might jazz up a newly orphaned child.

"Anastasia," Prim said, "you're going to live here with us!"

That night, locked once more in Room Eleven, motherless, fatherless, and guinea-pig-less, Anastasia lay in the child-shaped hollow and watched shadows slink across the ceiling. Tears twinkled in the corners of her eyes and slid down her cheeks and crept into her ears. From somewhere in the house crooned a noise like *EEEEEEE-ooooooooooaaaa*.

Of course, it was just St. Agony's settling into its foundations, like a lady with a large rump trying to squeeze into her bikini bottoms. Or perhaps it was wind whipping down the chimneys and groaning in the fireplaces. Or it could even have been a lonely owl, trapped in one of the dusty, abandoned rooms.

But Anastasia liked to think the house was crying with her.

They cried together all night.

It was a splendid day for a funeral. The ground squelched with mud, and clouds clotted the sky. Anastasia watched raindrops pimpling the puddles and nodded grimly. Very funereal weather.

It was the day after the aunties' dreadful announcement. After another breakfast of Mystery Lumps beneath Beauregard's lupine glare, Anastasia had followed her aunties up a spiraling stairwell to the top of the tallest of all the tall towers jutting from the roof. The tower had floor-to-ceiling windows on each of its eight walls. It would have afforded a lovely view of St. Agony's grounds, if St. Agony's grounds had been in any way lovely. Instead the tower overlooked mud and thistle and wonky bushes and a swampy pond that the aunties called a bog.

"Mud and Thistle," Anastasia whispered.

"What's that, dearie?" Prim asked.

"Nothing," Anastasia said. "Just thinking."

She was thinking of Prim's dream to someday convert the dreary asylum into a quaint bed-and-breakfast. Anastasia already had plenty of catchy names for it: The Mud 'n' Thistle. The Chill 'n' Molder. The Smell 'n' Shudder Inn.

"Such a peculiar girl," Prim said as she and Prude settled into two rickety rocking chairs. Prim rummaged in her purse for the lump of pink wool. Her knitting needles began to tick. Prude pulled a pair of binoculars out of her coat and held them over her nose.

"What are those for?" Anastasia asked.

"Bird-watching," Prude replied. "My little hobby. Last Tuesday I spotted a red-speckled twit! A real triumph!"

Wondering how Prude could possibly see any birds through the drizzle, Anastasia stared down at the blur of sludge and woods surrounding them. The poodles gallivanted among the scruffy topiaries.

"Do your poodles like to play?" she asked hopefully.

Prim chuckled. "Yes," she said, "but I expect you wouldn't like to play with them."

"They're not really pets, dear," Prude spoke up. "They're guard dogs."

As you may already know, Reader, poodles weren't bred to wear twinkly collars and lollygag in the teacups of wealthy ladies. Poodles were engineered to hunt and fight. They guarded sheep from wolves, which gives you a sense of how truly fearsome a full-sized poodle may be, even when trimmed and shaved and beribboned.

"Well, maybe I could make friends with them," Anastasia said. "Do you have any treats? Do you have cheese? My neighbor's Labradoodle will do tricks for cheese. Dogs love it."

"Indeed they do," Prim said. "But cheese gives dogs terrible flatulence. And life, my dear child, is difficult enough without having gassy poodles."

Anastasia turned away from the window. "When are we going to have the funeral?"

The knitting needles stopped. "Oh, dear," Prim said.

Prude lowered her binoculars. "Anastasia, funerals are ever so expensive."

"Oh, our poor moppet." Prim set aside her knitting and patted her lap. "Come up here with me."

Anastasia eyed the rocking chair doubtfully, then went over and wedged herself down beside her auntie. Prim slid her arm around Anastasia's shoulders. The fur sleeve prickled against her ears.

"I'm afraid we don't have the money for a funeral," said Prim. "Just *one* coffin would cost more than we have in our piggy bank."

"Not to mention the flowers and the cold-cut buffet," said Prude.

"Cold-cut buffet?" Anastasia repeated.

"You can't have a funeral without a cold-cut buffet," Prude said. "Mourners expect salami."

The itchy sleeve squeezed Anastasia. She started to slide out of the chair, but Prim said, "Now, now, don't go running off just yet. Your auntie Prude and I have something for you."

"A gift," Prude said. She reached into her fur coat and pulled out a little case.

"Go ahead," Prim said, smiling. "Open your present."

Coiled in the box, nestled against a square of velvet, lay a tarnished silver chain with a little heart.

"It was your great-grandmother McCrumpet's," Prude said. "Our mother's necklace, that is. We were going to give it to your mother one day, but—well—oh, dear . . ." She groped for her handkerchief. "We never got the chance."

"It's a family heirloom," Prim snuffled. "Let me fasten it for you." She plucked the box from Anastasia's grasp, a flash of silver glinting from her pinkie.

Anastasia's forehead crinkled. "You have that eyeball ring, too."

"Oh, yes," Prim said. "Isn't it pretty? Now hold still."

Anastasia trembled as her auntie fumbled with the clip. "Your hands are so cold, Auntie!"

"All old ladies have cold hands," Prim said. "It's because our hearts are weak and our blood runs slow and cold as swamp water in winter. There."

"Don't you look darling!" Prude exclaimed. "How does it feel?"

"Fine, I guess." Anastasia peered down at the charm. A tiny red dot winked at its center, like a little bloodshot eye.

"That's a real ruby," Prim said.

"Oh," Anastasia said. "Thank you." She forced a lopsided smile. Of course, Anastasia didn't really care about an old necklace. She just wanted to be by herself and think about her parents and Muffy. But she also knew that her aunties were trying to cheer her up, and that she couldn't disappoint them or they might send her to the orphanage. They had, over breakfast that morning, told her all about what happened in orphanages.

"Don't lose it," Prude warned. "It's very valuable."

"I won't." Anastasia tucked the necklace back into her collar. "You know, funerals don't have to be fancy," she said. "When Betty Lou died, we just stood by the compost heap and said some nice things about her."

"Who in heaven's name is Betty Lou?" Prim asked.

"Never mind." Anastasia wriggled out of the rocker and returned to the window. It was, she observed again, a splendid day for a funeral.

7

Leeches

ANASTASIA SOON DISCOVERED that *every* day at St. Agony's Asylum was perfect funeral weather. Standing outside one week later, after seven days of rain and fog, she blinked through the twilit mizzle at the moss fuzzing the asylum bog.

"Come on, dearie," Prim called from beneath her umbrella. "Those leeches aren't going to stroll up and introduce themselves, you know!"

"All right, all right." The ground squished as Anastasia sat down to pull off her boots, two old green galoshes she had found in one of the asylum's innumerable jumbled cupboards. They were about a size too big, but galoshes were better than her worn sneakers for trudging around the soggy asylum and its muddy gardens.

She struggled to her feet (*squish! squish!*) and shrugged out of her coat, a fur from the wardrobe in Room Eleven. It smelled like a wet Labradoodle (and as you already know, Anastasia disapproved of fur coats), but she needed something warm to wear. The aunties promised they would soon make the trip back to Mooselick to fetch some of her clothes and books, but it seemed the pink station wagon wouldn't start. In the meantime, Anastasia was stuck wearing her Halloween costume and the odiferous coat. Or, in this particular moment, she was stuck wearing a mildewed Victorian swimming suit she had discovered in a trunk.

"You're shilly-shallying, dear," Prim said.

They both stared at the bog.

"Why do I have to catch leeches, again?" Anastasia asked.

"Because they're worth money," Prim said. "You know we aunties are poor as church mice. And now that we have to take care of you, we can hardly even pay for our heart medicine. Both Prudence and I have such fragile hearts. You wouldn't want us to keel over and die, would you? Then you'd have to go to the orphanage after all."

Anastasia summoned all her gumption and dipped one toe into the slime. She leapt into the air with a shriek. "It's freezing!"

"Nonsense," Prim said. "It's brisk and refreshing. You

know, most orphans would be delighted to have a swimming pool right in their own backyard."

"This isn't a swimming pool," Anastasia muttered. "It's a bog."

"Stop splitting hairs," Prim said. "It's a first-rate bog. I don't know of a single orphanage with a bog half as fine as this one." She took a sip of tea from a chipped china cup. The teapot teetered on a nearby tree stump.

Anastasia stepped in with both feet, cringing as mud squidged between her toes. She inched forward. The bog was tooth-rattling cold. Goose bumps sprang up all over her body.

"Hurry," Prim called. "Chilly weather is very hard on us little old ladies, you know." She sipped her tea.

Mossy water seeped into the lace trimming Anastasia's Victorian pantaloons. "What about your Gardener?" she complained. "Why can't he do this? Where *is* he, anyway? I haven't even seen him since the night you whacked him with your umbrella." Her tummy somersaulted as she thought back to the authentic Victorian birdcage rattling against her car window. *Tingalingalingaling.* She didn't particularly crave another meeting with the lunatic Gardener, but she also didn't want to do all the nasty jobs required to maintain a rambling and ramshackle insane asylum.

"He's sick in bed. Delicate lungs, you know." Prim pulled a pickle from her coat pocket and champed into it. "Besides, you could benefit from a little exercise. Children need to frolic."

"Frolic?" Anastasia grumbled.

"St. Agony's is a charming asylum, but it isn't equipped with a gymnasium," Prim said. "You'll have to get your frolics from chores. Now wade around, dear. You have to give the leeches a fair chance to bite onto your legs."

"Will it hurt?"

"I've told you already, you won't feel a thing," Prim said. "Very courteous biters, leeches are. Unlike the Gardener, whom you'd do best to avoid."

Bog water oozed up to Anastasia's waist. She mucked forth, thinking about her father, and about their last funeral together, the morning of the fatal freak vacuuming accident that had changed everything.

By now, all the plants in the abandoned McCrumpet household would certainly be withered into lifeless husks. The bed where Mrs. McCrumpet had spent her days swigging cough syrup lay empty. Muffy had gone to a rodent orphanage, despite Anastasia's passionate protests. Everything in her life had changed with six little words: "Your mommy and daddy are dead."

For the first few days, Anastasia had wandered around St. Agony's in a haze. Part of her was convinced that Prim and Prude were wrong about her parents. It was just a horrible mistake. A hospital mix-up. A typo in the fateful telegram that arrived in the dark hours of the rainiest day of the year. But as the week dragged by and no one arrived on the mirrored stoop of St. Agony's to whisk Anastasia back to Mooselick, she slowly came to the conclusion that it was true: her parents were gone, and her home was now with her aunties.

She swiveled her eyes to the asylum and went stock-still. Behind the glass of a North Wing window crept a black-clad figure, the silver birdcage atop his shoulders gleaming in the twilight.

"Don't stop, child," Prim said. "Keep moving about."

"But I saw—"

"What?" Prim twisted her head. "There's nothing there, my dear."

"But—" Anastasia looked back up to the window. The silhouette was gone.

She sludged deeper into the bog. Why was the Gardener roaming the North Wing? It was off-limits. And wasn't he supposed to be ailing and abed? She scowled. Perhaps he was just playing sick to dodge his chores.

"Now, the more leeches that latch on to you, the better," Prim reminded her.

"Why do people buy leeches?" Anastasia asked. "Do they keep them for pets?"

"Of course not!" Prim said. "What kind of goon would love a leech?"

"Then who buys them?"

"Doctors," Prim replied. "Dr. Lipwig down in the village uses leeches for all sorts of important things. I hear he cured poor Mrs. O'Golly's gout with leeches. It's an authentic Victorian practice, you know."

It's true: Victorian doctors used to stick bloodsucking leeches on their rich and wretched patients in the hopes of curing their ailments. Why use leeches on *rich* patients, you may ask, and not *poor* ones? It may interest you to know that leeches were a luxury item in Victorian times. Butlers and cooks, a carriage with horses, and a nice big jarful of leeches—all part and parcel of the grand Victorian dream.

"Apparently that's why the founders of St. Agony's chose this spot for their splendid asylum," Prim went on. "Plenty of leeches for the taking. A bog like this is a real perk."

Anastasia slogged along, her gaze twitching to the neglected topiary bushes looming around them. The topiaries had once frolicked through the garden as whimsical animals but had long since swelled into shaggy, amorphous beasts. She glowered at them, and then she glowered at the glinting spikes of the electric fence girdling her aunties' property. She wondered whether the Gardener ever ventured through the heavy iron gates into the Dread Woods. Prim and Prude certainly didn't.

"You mustn't let the woods scare you *too* terribly, dear," Prim called.

"I'm *not* scared of the woods," Anastasia said, watching fog curl between the black tree trunks. "Are *you*?"

She couldn't see her auntie's eyes behind the clouded lenses of her spectacles, but she thought Prim's hands trembled. Of course, Prim's hands always trembled. "Not at all," Prim said. "We're very safe here. We have the electric fence, and besides, we have the poodles." She chuckled as a swarm of snarling wool crashed between the topiaries. "Oh, look! Cookie's got a squirrel!"

Anastasia cringed and made an addition to her list of bed-and-breakfast names: The Chomp 'n' Kill. She peered at the fluffy tail dangling from the dog's jaws. "Does Cookie have *metal* teeth?"

"Yes," Prim replied. "All our poodles do. Their breed is plagued with rotten gums. All their teeth fell out back when they were puppies, I'm sorry to say."

"Can I come out now?" Anastasia pleaded. "I can hardly feel my legs anymore."

"It *is* getting dark," Prim conceded. "All right. I suppose that will do for now." She slugged down the rest of her tea in one gulp and plunked the teacup into her purse.

Anastasia lumbered out of the bog, and Prim clasped her hands together in delight. "A fine harvest!"

Anastasia stared down at her legs. Dozens of leeches dangled from her shins and kneecaps. She reached to pluck one off.

"Ah ah ah!" Prim scolded. "Let them fall off when they've drunk their fill. Don't worry, they won't suck too much of your blood. Only about a teaspoon or so apiece."

"That's a lot of teaspoons!"

"You should be thanking me," Prim said. "You're getting a free bloodletting. Dr. Lipwig charges his patients good money for this."

Anastasia was too cold to argue. She struggled into her fur coat and waited for the leeches to finish their dinner. As each leech plopped from her leg with a satisfied sigh, Prim snatched it up and dropped it into her chilly teapot. Finally, when the last one had finished snacking, Anastasia pulled on her galoshes, and they began the uphill trudge to the asylum.

The final smidgens of sunlight fizzled away, steeping the gardens in shadow. Anastasia quickened her pace. *Thup! Pbbbt!* Her too-big galoshes made rude squashy noises in the thick mud. *Blaaat!*

"Was that you?" Prim gasped. "Did you make those dreadful sounds? Nice Little Girls don't do that."

"*I* didn't," Anastasia protested. "My boots did."

"What if you made one of those nasty noises in the middle of tea with a duchess?" Prim said. "What then?"

"I never drink tea with duchesses," Anastasia pointed out.

"Perhaps you will one day," Prim said. "One day, when you're a Nice Little Lady."

Anastasia shuddered, picturing herself as her aunties' idea of a Nice Little Lady. Sipping tea in a dusty parlor. Clutching a purse full of stale peppermint candies. Awful! Besides, she had other aspirations. As you already know, Anastasia planned to be a capable detective-veterinarian-artist when she grew up.

"That is, if you ever grow up at all," Prim was saying softly, almost to her herself.

"What?" Anastasia asked. "What did you just say?"

"Oh," Prim said, fumbling as her glasses fell off her nose and disappeared into the bristles of her fur collar. "Nothing, dear." She picked them up and put them back on her face, then blinked at Anastasia. Her eyes were cloudier than ever, like water into which one has spat toothpaste.

"What did you mean, *if I ever grow up*?" Anastasia persisted.

"It's just," said her auntie, "that life is very uncertain, isn't it?"

She smiled at Anastasia, and they went back into the asylum.

8

Eyeballs

AUNTIE PRIM IS right, good Reader: life is uncertain indeed. For example, you may be a perfectly average (if tragically flatulent) fifth grader at Mooselick Elementary School on Tuesday morning, and by Thursday afternoon you could find yourself scouring chamber pots at an authentically creepy Victorian mansion in the middle of nowhere, much like the most wretched of fairy-tale orphans.

Because her aunties were ancient prunes with fragile hearts, Anastasia was stuck with the struggles of maintaining a dilapidated mansion. And St. Agony's Asylum was in the throes of dilapidation, from its creaking towers to the dusty glass eyeballs staring from the animal trophies lining the walls. These marble eyeballs, in fact, were constantly coming unglued from their respective faces and plummeting to the floor. Every time Anastasia heard the telltale plunk of a kamikaze marble, she chased it down and dropped it into her satchel. She acquired her seventh marble the morning of the Incident at the Breakfast Table, which occurred shortly before she surprised herself with a Strange and Impulsive Act, all on the very same day she made a Most Mysterious Discovery.

It began like any other a.m. at the asylum: the aunties were yattering about bird-watching (*"Two* yellow-bellied sapsuckers? You don't say!"), and Anastasia was silently munching her Mystery Lumps, missing her father and his waffles from the bottom of her almost-eleven-year-old heart.

"Anastasia." Prim broke into her thoughts. "There's a nasty colony of spiderwebs in the Great Hall. Won't you be a dear?" Which was Auntie Code for *Clean it up and don't complain, because after all it's better than the orphanage!*

Anastasia groaned. "Is the Gardener still sick? Couldn't he do it?"

"As a matter of fact," Prim said, "our resident lunatic biter is up and about, but he has his own to-do list."

"And you really mustn't go near him," Prude said. "The cage helps with the biting, but he still scratches."

"Teenagers." Prude shuddered. "Beastly." She plunked a handful of sugar cubes into her tea.

Perhaps it was the dampness creeping through the asylum that loosened the glue. Or perhaps taxidermy paste only lasts a century or so. Whatever the reason, one marble eye-ball leapt from Beauregard's furry brow at the very moment that Prude lifted her teacup to her lips.

Zing! PLUNK! Sploosh!

"Gllrg!" Prude spluttered.

"Pardon me, Prudence?" Prim asked. She had not observed the marble's great nosedive. "I didn't quite hear you. It sounded like you said *gllrg.* And *gllrg* is not, I am quite certain, a word."

Prude wiped the lenses of her spectacles and peered down into her cup.

"WOLF!"

The teacup went flying across the dining room and smashed into smithereens against the wall. The green marble rolled away.

"What's come over you, Prudence?" Prim cried. "Are you having some kind of fit?"

"There was," Prude wheezed, "an eyeball . . . in my tea-cup."

"Impossible," Prim declared. "I strained that tea myself. I would have noticed an—er—errant eyeball."

"Green, it was, and staring right at me!" Prude insisted. "Green, like the eyes of a wolf!"

"You must be imagining things," Prim said. "Your mind is playing tricks on you. It's the worry of caring for an orphan. Speaking of orphans—Anastasia, dear?"

"The cobwebs," Anastasia muttered. "I know."

Leaving her Mystery Lumps uneaten, she scurried into the Great Hall and tracked down Beauregard's glass peeper. She plucked it up between her thumb and forefinger.

EeeeeeeOOoooooooooo.

Hark!

Could it be the wind shrilling in St. Agony's flues, doing a splendid imitation of whale song?

Eeeeoooooowwwwwoo.

The wuthering *was* rather like a song. Anastasia felt there was some sort of melody to it, and she now knew it by heart.

Eeeeeeooooeeeeee.

Did the chimneys pipe music through the asylum like some kind of inside-out church organ? Anastasia's eyes slid toward the window. The trees of the Dread Woods were still, fog petticoating their dark trunks. There was no wind.

She plunked the marble into her satchel and crept between the sheeted whatnots to the parlor adjoining the Great Hall. The fireplace mantel sagged beneath a pair of cobweb-swaddled candelabra. Anastasia leapfrogged the grate and ducked into the hearth, peering up. Something was jamming the flue. She grasped the edges, grimacing as soot cascaded onto her head, and pried the blockage loose. As the smoggy cloud puffed itself out, pale light traced a row of iron rungs leading up the chimney's gullet to a square of gray sky high above.

You might wonder whether the builders of St. Agony's Asylum thoughtfully fitted their chimney with this peculiar ladder on Santa Claus's behalf. However, the rungs in the flue served a purpose far less jolly. They were installed for the chimney sweeps that mucked out the flues of Victorian homes. And, you will be shocked to learn, Victorians often employed children *younger than you* for this dangerous and filthy task.

Why *children*? Because, dear Reader, children are small. Children can fit into tight places where adults dare not venture.

Eeeeeoooooooooooeeee.

Anastasia hurdled back over the grate, shaking her braids. The ghostly noise wasn't coming from the chimneys. And, she reasoned, it wasn't the poodles yodeling for a snack, either. The sound was coming from *inside* the asylum; she was sure of it. She studied the sooty doodad plundered from the chimney's throat. Why in crumbs would anyone shove a mirror inside a chimney?

"Anastasia," Prim warbled. "Where are you, moppet?"

Anastasia crammed the looking glass behind a curtain and hustled back to the Great Hall.

"Here you are!" Prim rounded the corner. "Why didn't you answer me?"

"Sorry, Auntie." Anastasia tweaked a dust bunny from a statuette's snoot. "Were you calling me?"

"I just wanted to make sure that you were at your chores," Prim twittered.

"Yep," Anastasia said. "Hard at work."

"Goody," Prim said. "Such a Nice Little Girl. Now give Auntie a kiss before I go up to my knitting."

Anastasia reluctantly pressed her lips to Prim's crinkled cheek. As she pulled away, the old woman shuddered. Her auntie must be cold. Prim's eyes slithered over her.

She patted Anastasia's braid, and then tugged on the chain of Great-Granny McCrumpet's necklace. "You're being careful with this, I hope? Is that a rash I see on your neck?"

"No," Anastasia said. "Those are freckles."

"And quite a bit of dirt, too," Prim clucked. "Perhaps you should take another dunk in the bog?"

"I don't mind a little dirt," Anastasia said hastily.

"That's very fortunate," Prim said, "because there's ever so much work to do around this place. Don't forget about those horrid cobwebs." She disappeared into the asylum.

Anastasia eyed the webs festooning the Great Hall. Where to begin? She contemplated the paintings above the stairs. Perhaps she would discover a priceless masterpiece beneath the grime, and her aunties could auction it off and hire a lunatic maid to tackle the gruesome asylum chores.

She yanked a ratty sock from her coat pocket and clumped up to the first artwork. "Waffle crumbs and coffee cake crumbs!" she groused, swiping at the cobwebs drooping from the picture frame. "Oh, hello. Poor you," she greeted a moth struggling in one of the silken snares. "Let me help you."

Now, I'm sure you have seen nature films in which, for example, a chameleon unfurls its magnificent long tongue to lasso a fly, or a bat swoops upon a whizzing insect, or a nimble tree frog leaps upon its prey and chomps it faster than you can wink. It all happens with astonishing speed. The producers of the nature show may even slow the film down, in order for our slow human eyes to catch the lightning-quick movements of other species.

As Anastasia reached for the insect trapped in the spiderweb, time went all funny, and she saw her hands move as though she were watching one of those fascinating nature films. She watched one fur-sleeved arm shoot out. She watched the freckled hand on the end of this arm close its fingers around the moth. The hand then swooped up to her mouth in a swift arc, her lips opened, and in went the moth. Anastasia's teeth were already crunching her fuzzy victim before her brain realized what she had done.

"*Paaah!*" She spat the moth onto the palm of her hand. The creature fluttered its tattered wings once or twice, gave a "goodbye, cruel world" sort of sigh, and lay still.

The poor fellow was dead as a dormouse.

Horror flooded through Anastasia. What had possessed her to eat an innocent moth? Was constant hunger driving her to desperate deeds of moth munching? For Anastasia *was* constantly hungry. Two bowls of Mystery Lumps per day were certainly not enough to nourish a growing, almost-eleven-year-old girl. She did not even get dinner. Anastasia's tummy grumbled its discontent as regularly as a grumpy grandfather clock. But what could she do about it? Prim and Prude kept the kitchen door locked.

"There are all kinds of dangerous things in the kitchen," Prim had explained. "Knives and forks and sporks. Children come to bad ends with sporks!"

"And the oven," Prude fretted. "Ooooh, the oven. What if you were to fall inside? That, my child, would be very painful indeed."

"We know that you're hungry, but we can hardly afford to feed you as it is," Prude told her mournfully. "We had no idea that orphans ate so much!"

Anastasia looked around, just to see whether anyone had observed her Strange and Impulsive Act. She was quite alone.

The moth lolled on her palm.

Without even thinking *ready-steady-go!* she gulped the bug down. Then she returned her attention to cleaning, trying very hard not to think about the bizarre (and rather unveterinarian-like) thing she had just done.

Anastasia whisked the old sock (formerly her flying-squirrel tail) across the canvas. *Swish.* The years of dust swirled away. *Swish. Swish.* The painted frump materialized. A black hat puffed like an enormous meringue atop her head; a swath of lace drooping from the brim cloaked her face down to her scowl. Leaning forward, Anastasia could just detect a fierce blond monobrow beneath the pattern of dark rosettes.

Swish. The dust avalanched from the background, revealing carefully daubed-in wallpaper. It was, she noticed, the same dreary floral design that splotched the asylum walls from floor to ceiling. Had, once upon a time, this monobrowed damsel lived in St. Agony's? Anastasia brandished her sock. *Swish.* A ribbon cinched the woman's waist, and affixed to this ribbon was an ornate clasp dangling with delicate chains. A thin metal box hung from one chain; a tiny pocket watch swung from another; a little bottle glittered at the end of a third chain; and finally, suspended from the last sterling strand, there was a fancy key, all silver curls and loops.

Anastasia licked the tip of her finger and scrubbed at the painted key. As the grime dissolved beneath her potent drool, she could distinguish a number squeezed amidst the filigree.

"Thirteen!" she said. "Bad luck!" She scrutinized the dour maiden. "Is that why you look so crusty? Were you unlucky?"

Miss Crusty, of course, remained silent.

Anastasia smeared her sock across the portrait once more. She froze.

A ring inscribed with the glowering eyeball symbol gleamed, in silver paint, on the damsel's pinkie. Anastasia boggled. It was the same ring Miss Sneed had been wearing. It was the same ring glinting on the pinkies of both her ancient aunties.

Peculiar, to say the least! Goose bumps prickled Anastasia's neck as she beheld the glaring eye. She swallowed and galoshed up to the next painting. Her heart thumped as she attacked the dust gloving the portrait-sitter's hand. *"Son of a biscuit!"*

She raced up the stairs, peeling back the cobwebs from the next five paintings. Five silver rings on five pinkies!

Panting, she scaled the top step to the last portrait, exclaiming under her breath at her final pinkie-ring sighting. Anastasia studied the meaty hand with a feeling like ice creeping through her veins.

Standing on tippy-toes, she stretched the sock up. With one swift motion, Anastasia exposed the woman's forehead and confirmed her suspicions.

"The Monobrow," she whispered.

Locked into her room that night, Anastasia lay in the child-shaped hollow and pondered her Most Mysterious Discovery. What was the meaning of the sinister eyeball symbol? And why did all the women in the portraits have monobrows? For, after smearing the dust from the horrible forehead of Miss Sneed's likeness, Anastasia had inspected the other paintings. Each canvas featured a woman upon whose forehead bristled a sinister monobrow.

Was the eyeball ring a hideous family heirloom passed down through the monobrowed generations?

But that couldn't be right, because Anastasia distinctly remembered her aunties saying that they had ordered their rings from the shopping channel on television. Besides, Miss Sneed had one of the rings, too. And why on earth was there a portrait of Miss Sneed hanging in St. Agony's Asylum?

Eeeeeeeeeooooooooooooo.

And *what* was making those ghostly wailing sounds? Anastasia hugged Mr. Bunster, foreboding pickling her thoughts. Something suspicious was festering within St. Agony's walls. Something rank and rotten. Anastasia could practically *smell* it. "Mr. Bunster," she muttered, "something *stinks.*"

EeeeeeEEEeeeeooooeeeeee.

She knew from experience that questioning her aunties

did not produce satisfactory results. For example, if she were to say the next morning at breakfast, "Aunties, why is there a painting of the Mooselick Elementary School secretary in your stairwell?" she would receive one or more of the following maddening responses:

1. "Whatever do you mean, moppet? Your school secretary, you say? You must be imagining things."
2. "Goodness me, is that a ruby-throated cuckoo? Oh, this *is* thrilling! Anastasia, dear, we're a bit busy."
3. "Nice Little Girls don't talk with their mouths full."

And so forth.

It would be the same if she asked about the rings or the peculiar music. She would get answers that weren't really answers at all. If Anastasia wanted the nitty-gritty on the mysteries stinking up the Asylum, she would have to whiff it out herself. That, she told herself firmly, was what Francie Dewdrop would do.

"Tomorrow, Mr. Bunster," she vowed, "I will launch my first great detective investigation."

✤ 9 ✤

View Through a Keyhole

LAUNCHING A GREAT detective investigation in a rickety Victorian mansion is not a task upon which to embark lightly, dear Reader. Prim and Prude were not whistling Dixie, Anastasia knew, when they pointed out that many of the asylum's clammy pockets were neither safe nor healthy places in which to roam. Some of the rooms were so damp that Moose-Spattered Toadstools sprouted in the soggy corners, and Perpetual Ooze Moss crept across the tattered wallpaper like algae on the sides of a neglected aquarium. The pink carpet squished underfoot like sponge cake, and black widow spiders bungee jumped from the cobwebbed chandeliers. The lunatic Gardener was on the loose, too.

However, while murk and moss and a tooth-gnashing Gardener were horrifying prospects indeed, Anastasia was an aspiring detective-veterinarian-artist. Aspiring detective-veterinarian-artists thrived in dilapidated mansions.

Having read every single Francie Dewdrop mystery, from *The Conundrum at Mildew Manor* to *The Riddle of the Whispering Tree*, Anastasia knew all sorts of detective tricks. She knew that a good sleuth noticed everything, even teensy little details like a button lying on the floor or mud spattered on a trouser cuff. She knew about sneaking and tiptoeing, listening at doorways, and hiding in cupboards. She had learned in chapters seven through eleven of *The Mystery of the Mercurial Garden* that locked rooms and forbidden drawers yielded clues as dark and delicious as triple-chocolate cake.

Anastasia reckoned she could sniff out these delicious clue crumbs during the hours she normally spent cleaning the asylum—after breakfast each morning, when the aunties trotted up to their glass tower to knit lumpy shawls and spy on twee-tufted bog warblers, and then after lunch until bedtime. *Good old-fashioned exercise*, the aunties called their never-ending list of asylum drudgery. *You'll have to get your frolics from chores*, Prim had told her. Well, unbeknownst to her aunties, Anastasia would henceforth get her frolics from detective work.

She spent the first days of her great investigation creeping around the rooms of the West Wing. What exactly, you may ask, was our intrepid sleuth seeking? Anastasia suspected that Miss Crusty had lived in the asylum, and wondered whether

she had left behind some sort of hint to the meaning behind
the uncanny eyeball rings. Perchance the silver clasp and its
curious charms were slumbering on a pillow of mold in one
of the madhouse's neglected chambers. Anastasia wanted to
find the fancy key engraved with number thirteen, and she
hoped she would find the door it unlocked.

She tripped over tarnished mirrors bolted to the floors
in the doorways. She plundered a credenza in Room Eight,
finding a marvelous old magnifying glass. In Room Nine-
teen, she discovered a curio cabinet jam-packed with seashells. Hefting a pink-lipped conch from its ledge, she held
it to her ear and closed her eyes.

Shhhhhhh . . .

. . . shhhh . . . shhhhh . . .

Anastasia knew the shushing was really the murmurations

hiding a *lot* of secrets. Her hat

lace the phrenology head in its
he gold-stamped spines of books
the cobweb clouds with a swipe
the wall was crammed with old
ide to side, and her heart pitter-
pation.

ncie Dewdrop's thrilling adven-
e regularly discovers bookshelves
ageways. During her escapades,
se heavy dictionaries and press-
ated no less than twenty clock-
aside to reveal secret vestibules

fully studied each and every one
reasoned that a vast mysterious
sylum should, by all rights, pos-
al bookcase.

or concealed buttons.

their ledges.

to the floor, eyeing the embossed
gruesome titles such as *Mushy*,
nal Society of Nutcase Study's Find-
d *Dr. Vagueworth's Monograph on*

and sighs and other hundreds of tiny noises that fill up a quiet house, amplified and ricocheting inside the shell. But she could almost imagine the sea was mumbling to her. She even fancied she could hear the faraway sound of a whale singing . . . *eeeeeOOOOOOeeee* . . .

The wobbly wailing music! She thunked the shell back on its shelf and dashed into the hallway. *EEEEEEOOOOOooo.* She cocked her head, then darted down a twisting side passage. *Ooooooowwwwww.* Left! *Eeeeeeooooo.* Right! Left again! *OOOOOeeeeeeeee . . . eee.* She strained her eardrums.

But the weird melody had faded.

The itty-bitty hairs along her nape prickling like a spooked hedgehog's quills, Anastasia gazed down the hall. Might the source of the haunted music be lurking behind one of the dark corridor's dozens of closed doors?

Nibbling her lower lip, she bore her candle and its tiny beacon through the nearest doorway.

Dust-cloaked furniture swelled around her like snow-mantled hills, and cobwebs billowed over the walls like cirrus clouds. Anastasia slunk deeper into this peculiar hinterland, her pupils drinking the gloom. She didn't detect anything that could have produced the whale sounds, but she did spot a mammoth rolltop desk. Might Miss Crusty have cached the key to Room Thirteen in one of the bureau's pigeonholes?

Anastasia hoisted the wooden lip.

The bureau spat out a dark, fluttering, buzzing, mumbling whirlwind. *Moths!* She pirouetted, tailing one fuzzy colossus into the far depths of the lightless room, where the critter bumbled into the pale froth of a cobweb drooping from a shelf.

"I'm sorry," Anastasia told it, her heart panging. "But I'm so hungry. Back in Mooselick, I would *never* have eaten you. I much prefer waffles."

As she reached forth to nab her fuzzy prey, her candlelight tickled the edges of a shadow lurking behind the rotten spider silk. Her hand froze.

It was a disembodied head.

Anastasia's candle clattered to the floor. She plowed backward into a warped grandfather clock, startling it into a rusty coughing fit. *BONG! BONG! BONG!* Panicked, she flung open the clock's glass breast and stilled its long golden tongue. *BONNNNG!*

If so, Miss Crusty was *enormous.*

As she stretched to niche, Anastasia glimpse lining the shelf. Scatteri of her sleeve, she saw th books, floor to ceiling ar pattered with sudden ant

If you have followed tures, you will know that that pivot into hidden p Francie had, by tugging ing cunning switches, ac work bookcases that sli chock-full of dandy clues.

Anastasia, who had ca of Francie's fantastic find mansion like St. Agony's sess at least one such mag

She combed the walls
She nudged tomes fro
Nothing happened.

Anastasia hopped dow book spines. They all bor *Pink, and Putrid: The Natio ings on Criminal Brains* an

New Fashions in Straitjacketry (The Curvy Silhouette). Shuddering, she pulled from the shelf *The Barber-Surgeon's Guide to the Latest Muttonchop and Self-Lobotomy Techniques.*

The pages were so warped from the mist that the letters inside had blurred into nonsense words like *grimwhiskerly* and *uneedledodo.* Anastasia let the dismal tome wheeze shut, yearning from the bottom of every freckle on her body to be back in the cheery library of Mooselick Elementary School, a Francie Dewdrop mystery on her lap and five (or six) of Miss Apple's scrumptious snickerdoodle cookies in her belly.

Tingalingaling!

Clutching the dreary volume, she cracked the library door and peeked out. The Gardener was pancaked against the corridor wall, creeping through the gloom, eyes shifting behind the bars of his birdcage. He edged into Room

Twenty-Four, scanning the hallway before pulling the door shut behind him.

It was Most Mysterious Behavior. And Anastasia found herself Incurably Curious. Her feet pattered of their own accord up the musty pink carpeting, and quick as you please, she knelt and squinted at the strange scene beyond the keyhole.

It was her first good look at the lunatic Gardener. She marveled at his raggedy, old-fashioned clothes—a velveteen jacket with tattered lapels, a waistcoat missing half its brass buttons, and too-short trousers that ended halfway between his knees and ankles, exposing green-and-white-striped socks. Did his employment contract with Prim and Prude include a clause requiring authentically shabby Victorian garb?

The boy prowled the room. "Hello," he whispered. *"Hellooooo."*

Anastasia's pulse juddered. Was he talking to himself?

The Gardener paused by a bell jar frosted with dust. "Are you in *here*?" He lifted the dome, revealing a somber stuffed owl. "Sorry, old boy. Didn't mean to disturb you." He replaced the lid. "Where *are* you?"

Had the Gardener, perhaps, lost a pet hamster?

He stalked to a fanciful glass terrarium shaped like a house and rapped one of its mossy walls. "Hello? Are you in here?" He raised the tiny roof and shook his head. "Nothing but toadstools."

Maybe, Anastasia thought, *he befriended one of the asylum's spiders.*

Suddenly the keyhole went dark. The door flew open, and the Gardener loomed over her. The bars of his birdcage prickled in her candlelight, and the bell rattled madly, screaming *Tingalingalingaling!*

"*You!*" he whispered. "*I've been looking for you!*"

❦ 10 ❦

A Peculiar Door

"**F**OR *ME?*" **ANASTASIA** squeaked, goggling up at the Gardener. He was so *tall*. A padlock dangled from the base of his silver coop, fastening his neck with a metal collar. As he crept forth, this padlock swung to and fro. Anastasia stared at it, nearly hypnotized with fear.

"We need to talk," the Gardener hissed.

"I—I have laryngitis." Anastasia mustered a cough worthy of her hypochondriac mom. "Maybe some other time."

"There might not be another time," he muttered.

"Don't come any closer!" Anastasia yelped. "Don't you *dare* bite me!"

"Bite you?" the Gardener echoed, seizing Anastasia's shoulders and sending her heart lolloping into her throat. "What did those old women tell you about me?"

"W-well," Anastasia stammered, "they might have mentioned something about a—um—a lunatic."

His fingers clenched tighter.

"But I'm sure they were talking about someone else," Anastasia gasped.

The Gardener leaned so close that the bars of his birdcage pressed painfully against her nose. "You and I are going to have a little chitchat," he whispered. "But don't you dare tell them I spoke to you, or we'll *both* be in trouble."

"Let me *go!*" Anastasia cried, wriggling her shoulders. *The Barber-Surgeon's Guide* plunged from her sweaty palms and crashed down to mash the tips of the Gardener's authentically scuffed Victorian shoes.

"Owwww!" he hollered. "My innocent toes!"

Anastasia wrenched out of his grasp and scrambled away into the labyrinth of corridors, galloping heck-for-leather until her lungs burned and her side panged and her legs joggled like jelly. Not even daring the teensiest backward glance, she vaulted a mirror bolted in the doorway to Room Nine and ducked inside.

Anastasia flopped onto a fainting couch, breathless and woozy. She was perilously close to crying, but she blinked her tears back. Francie Dewdrop didn't boohoo when threatened by goons. She touched the tip of her nose and winced. What revenge, she wondered, would the Gardener exact if she blabbed about the frightening exchange?

Well, she wasn't going to tell, anyway. Anastasia *couldn't* tell Prim and Prude about bumping into the Gardener, and not just because he had promised trouble. If her aunties reprimanded him, the barmcakes boy might tattle that Anastasia was snooping around the asylum's forbidden wings. And that, she knew, would bring her brilliant detective work to a screeching halt.

And Anastasia did not intend to stop investigating.

The cushions of the fainting couch were moldy and curled up at the corners like a cheese sandwich that has been toasted too long. Anastasia spied a glimmer between them and plunged her hand into the crevice.

She pulled out a petite silver bottle attached to a slender chain. Tiny script on the bottle read DR. MERRYMOOD'S SMELLING SALTS. Anastasia shook it and listened closely to the pebbly little rattle within, but she didn't pull out the fancy stopper.

Because would-be sickie Mrs. McCrumpet had consulted every expert medic and smooth-talking quack in Mooselick, Anastasia was familiar with many pills and syrups and cure-alls. For example, she knew that waving a bottle of smelling salts beneath someone's snoot is supposed to jozzle them awake. She even remembered that Victorian ladies, whose fanciful underwear squished their lungs and left them wobbly from oxygen deprivation, bought fainting couches upon which to swoon, and dangled little bottles of smelling salts from chains they wore at their waists.

Anastasia knew something else about the small silver flask. *It was Miss Crusty's bottle.* Victory zinged through her veins, sweet and bubbly as sarsaparilla, as she gazed upon her first major find as an aspiring detective-veterinarian-artist. But where were the silver clasp and the rest of its odd charms? She leapt up and flung the cushions off the sofa, then pushed her fingers into all the folds and creases. Nothing.

Crawling on her hands and knees, Anastasia inspected beneath the sofa. There, nestled among the dust bunnies, she found not the clasp but a block of Dr. Whistlewind's Miracle Choco-Laxative. Laxatives, in case you don't know, help you poop. She brushed the grime off the elegant paper wrapper. The Miracle Choco-Laxative had lain under the couch for a very long time. Probably a hundred years.

Anastasia sighed. No matter how her stomach growled, and no matter how her sweet tooth ached, she wasn't quite desperate enough to munch chocolate laxatives. She thrust the bar back beneath the fainting couch. Then, spying a flutter out of the corner of her eye, she snatched a moth from a cobweb and snarfed it down.

"*I'm* shocked, too," she informed the spider whose lunch she had just stolen. "Under normal circumstances, I would *never* eat a moth. It's creepy and weird. No offense."

Turning away from the spider's eight-eyed glare, Anastasia noticed a curious door in the wall. The door was square and small—perhaps just large enough for an almost-eleven-year-old girl to climb through—and, unlike most doors, it was smack-dab in the middle of the wall, right where one would normally hang a painting.

It was an intriguing door. It was the type of door a troll might use in a fairy tale. Anastasia stared at the door and wondered where it led.

Threading the chain of the smelling-salt bottle through one of her belt loops, she tromped across the parlor, opened the little door, and looked inside.

Her breath whistled against her front teeth.

"*Dumbwaiter,*" she whispered.

Dumbwaiters are similar to miniature elevators. A dumbwaiter is a box built between the walls, and one can move it up and down by pulling on a rope. In grand old houses of bygone eras, dumbwaiters were used to hoist food from the kitchen to other stories. A servant in a ruffled cap would place, for example, a figgy pudding into the dumbwaiter, and then heave the snack up to a hungry lord or lady or duke or duchess (or, in this case, criminally insane inmate) playing charades in a third-story parlor.

Anastasia had read about dumbwaiters in *The Conundrum at Mildew Manor*, so she had already considered the exciting potential of such a device. Staring into the cobwebby interior of the wooden dumbwaiter before her, ideas began to sprout in her mind like Moose-Spattered Toadstools. She could zip from floor to floor without meeting her aunties—or the Gardener—on the stairwells.

And perhaps she could even haul herself into some of the sealed wings of the asylum. Anastasia suspected that, in those hidden and abandoned places, she would find some sort of explanation to the asylum mysteries. Maybe the dumbwaiter would even take her to Room Thirteen.

She took a deep breath and splayed her hands on the base of the rickety wooden box. What if the ancient rope snapped and sent her plummeting to the bottom of the shaft? Nudging this unpleasant thought to the back of her mind, she hoisted herself inside and closed the little fairy door behind her.

Her arms were strong from weeks of scrubbing chamber pots and wrestling weeds from the ground and doing other nasty chores, but she still struggled and panted as she hauled the dumbwaiter slowly upward. The rope prickled against her hands. Finally she saw the outline of a door, faintly traced in pale—and strangely *greenish*—light. To her astonishment, smoke began to seep through this peculiar green seam.

Was the asylum on fire? Anastasia rammed the door with her shoulder, panic swelling her tonsils. The wood moaned but refused to budge. *Crumbs!* Twisting herself like a Bavarian pretzel, she placed the soles of her galoshes against the door and kicked with all her might. The door burst open and out tumbled Anastasia, hurdy-gurdy-head-over-heels-nose-over-toes-bum-over-teakettle, right into another of the asylum's mysterious armpits.

11

The Memories Book

ANASTASIA'S GAZE SEESAWED around the strange chamber into which she had somersaulted. Tall panes of green glass windowed the pointed walls.

She was in one of the asylum's many towers.

Green light seeped through the tinted windows, turning Anastasia's skin the color of an amphibious critter. A warped four-poster bed, cloaked in a mildewed canopy, loomed like a shipwreck amidst furniture swollen with a century of damp. And *fog*—not smoke—leaked into the tower room from a broken windowpane. The fog swirled across the floor, knee-deep, so that when Anastasia wobbled to her feet she could see neither her galoshes nor the squishy carpet into which they sank.

An arched doorway yawned into a dark stairwell.

Anastasia leaned to peek down the iron spiral and saw that, seven treads from the top, the metal coil had broken off completely. The only way to or from the tower was now the dumbwaiter.

She turned and waded deeper into the fog. Her green reflection quivering in the mirror above a vanity, she ransacked its drawers for a key or an errant eyeball ring or something else of interest. Finding only mildewed gloves, she moved to the wardrobe. She rustled through moth-eaten crinolines. She plunged her hands into pockets soggy with mold. Her eyebrows furrowed. According to Francie Dewdrop novels, deserted towers bore whiz-bang clues! She threw aside a moldy pair of bloomers, then snatched a moth from a cobweb and popped it into her mouth. It may astonish you, gentle Reader, to know that Anastasia was beginning to *like* moths. They were rather like fuzzy potato chips.

Glimpsing a brassbound trunk peeking from beneath the four-poster's dust ruffle, she twitched the bed skirt aside. She gazed in admiration at the rotting coffer for a moment before heaving the lid up a couple of inches.

Hundreds of teeny glass vials glinted in the green light. She plucked one up. Clear fluid swished inside. Anastasia frowned and replaced it, then carefully snaked her arm into the chest and rummaged until her fingers closed around a paper carton.

Miss Eelheart's Superior-Grade Tear Catchers
For the Demure Lady in Mourning
(Veil Not Included)

Anastasia opened the box. One empty vial rolled at the base. She held it between her thumb and forefinger, and then gazed down at the chest. How many prim and proper Victorian tears were bottled up and sealed away in this odd room? She slipped the tiny flask into her pocket, adding to her growing collection of Victorian oddities.

The tear catchers tinkled as Anastasia let the trunk's lid fall shut.

Then she spied it—on top of the wardrobe, hidden behind a bizarre collection of bell jars crammed with sticks, sat a pale pink hatbox.

She dragged the ruffled vanity stool across the room and climbed up on it, stretching her hands for the hatbox. Her fingertips brushed something else—a big book—and she heave-hoed until both tome and hatbox plummeted into her arms, knocking her off the stool and down into the fog. The hatbox rolled away.

"Crumb of a biscuit!" Clutching the book, Anastasia peeled herself from the floor and sank onto the vanity stool.

Her femurs groaned beneath the enormous album. It was bound in dark velveteen, with the word MEMORIES embroidered across the front.

The pages warped beneath her fingers. There were purple flowers squished flat beneath soggy tissue paper. There were locks of pale hair tied with ribbons gone black. Anastasia handled the pages with great delicacy, fearful they would dissolve if she even breathed on them. She thought of Miss Apple's frequent reminders to the students of Mooselick Elementary: "Turn these pages carefully, children, for you're holding someone's dreams!"

One hot, homesick tear crawled down Anastasia's cheek.

She wiped it away, blinking. There were several photographs of a weak-chinned man with muttonchops and a monocle, mooning over a twig perched on his palm. How curious. "To my darling Caterpillar Face," he had penned in green ink in the corner of one of these portraits. *Caterpillar Face?* Who would nickname their sweetheart Caterpillar Face?

She continued leafing through Caterpillar Face's album, passing over a section of pages gummy with pasted-in prints from old advertisements. Bustles! Girdles! A review for *Miss Drusilla Jellymonk's Etiquette Manual for the Prim and Proper Sort:* "A Practical Guide to Correct Behavior for Every Situation Imaginable, from Suitable Mourning Attire to the Polite Polishing of One's Glass Eye; from Selection of Superior Teatime Puddings to the Manifold Appropriate Uses for Orphans (e.g., Doorstops and Chimney Sweeps)."

Anastasia shivered, envisioning herself climbing up a rusted ladder like the one in the chimney downstairs. Thank goodness she wasn't a Victorian orphan! She quickly flipped past the ads to an obituary for Cornelius Clodfelter, of Withering Springs.

CELEBRATED ENTOMOLOGIST (BUG SCIENTIST, THAT IS) PERISHES FROM FATAL BLACK WIDOW BITE

"His passion," the obituary reported, *"was the rare Withering Springs Walking Stick, a clever insect known for impersonating twigs. He also had a thing for caterpillars."*

Anastasia swiveled her gaze to the glass jars of sticks. So they were specimens of stick insects and not, in fact, bundles of twigs. Had Caterpillar Face shed the trunkful of tears for Mr. Clodfelter? How very tragic.

She sighed and turned one of the last pages, then blinked with refreshed interest at the pasted-in newspaper articles. Tall, livid letters, their sides bleeding black into the yellowed paper, screamed: SCHOOLGIRL SNATCHED FROM SWEETSHOP STILL MISSING!

Another one, dated 1895: HEARTBROKEN MOTHER DESPAIRS AS SEARCH FOR SON PLODS ON!

1899: POLICE BAFFLED BY DISAPPEARANCE OF TEN-YEAR-OLD "GOLDILOCKS" TWINS!

Why would anyone collect such gloomy articles? Was the Victorian lady who clipped these headlines an aspiring detective, perhaps?

LINUS SHOETREE VANISHES FROM COUNTY FAIR!

GLUTTONOUS BOY SCAMPERS OFF TO BUY CANDY FLOSS; NEVER RETURNS!

A photograph of Linus's last moments with his family had been printed beneath the shocking headline. Anastasia took out her magnifying glass and held it over the picture. It was a marvel, she thought, how photos captured a split second in time. Eyelids crinkled, nostrils flaring, Linus would forevermore be petrified in the middle of sneezing on his old-timey sailor collar. The balloon man would, regrettably, always have one finger jammed up his nostril. The veiled woman in the background would be eternally tearing a fluff of cotton candy from the bag she clutched in her left hand—

The magnifying glass trembled over the face. Anastasia knew that scowl! *But how?* The clipping was more than a hundred years old! How could Anastasia have possibly seen this glowering fairgoer before?

She peered even closer.

A silver eyeball glared on the woman's pinkie.

Anastasia set the MEMORIES book atop the vanity with a dreadful feeling swimming in her tummy. Hands shaking, she fumbled in the fog for the hatbox and yanked off its round lid. Her stomach flip-flopped as she lifted the edges of a wide black brim drooping with lace.

It was the monstrous hat on the woman in the Great Hall portrait.

Miss Crusty was Caterpillar Face. So Cornelius Clodfelter, celebrated bug scientist, had fallen for her *monobrow*! Her bristly blond monobrow probably reminded him of yellow woolly bear caterpillars, Anastasia mused. And her bristly blond monobrow reminded Anastasia of something, too.

The fairgoer in the newspaper photograph.

Anastasia only needed one more glance through the magnifying glass to confirm her suspicions. Caterpillar Face from the asylum portrait was the woman hovering near Linus Shoetree just seconds before he vanished.

The hatbox rolled onto its side and gagged a froth of tissue paper into the fog. Something gleamed in its cardboard curve. Anastasia's pupils swelled and grasped the gleam. If you were staring into Anastasia's eyes at that moment, dear Reader, you would have seen mirrored in their black centers a silver clasp. You would have seen the tiny reflections of Anastasia's hands stretching toward the clasp and lifting it up, and you would have seen, swinging upon silver chains, a pocket watch and a little box.

The key was gone.

Crumbs! Crumbs to the nth power!

Anastasia's fingers tightened around the oversized brooch, and she gave it an angry shake. Then she set the clasp in her lap and examined the clock. She twisted the little pin at its top and cranked its gears, sending the dainty arrows twirling. After its century-long nap in the tower room, the silver timepiece woke up. *Tick tick tick tick tick.*

Anastasia squinted at the silver case. Fancy letters scrolling across its front spelled out *Calling Cards*. She shoved her thumbnail in the seam and prized it open.

There was still one card clipped inside:

❊ 12 ❊

Eavesdropping

BACK IN HER room, Anastasia copied the glowering eyeball symbol into her sketch pad. The pages were scribbled full of little drawings of St. Agony's Asylum. After her aunties twisted the key in the lock to Room Eleven each night at sundown, Anastasia had lots of time to sit and doodle. She had drawn careful homesick portraits of Muffy and Miss Apple. And, of course, she had drawn her father. Every evening before she curled into the child-shaped hollow in her cot, she opened her pad and stared at her pencil drawing of Fred McCrumpet. His mustache and right ear were blotchy from teardrops.

She had also sketched a few unflattering caricatures of her aunties.

Perhaps you have a relative whom you don't really like.

An uncle who screeches with laughter at his own unfunny jokes, or a cousin who tattles the second she finds firecrackers stashed under your bed. Or maybe a grandma who insists on kissing you even though her chin is bristlier than a cactus on steroids.

If anyone had asked Anastasia whether she actually liked her aunties, she would have politely answered that yes, of course she did. But deep down, in the deepest corner of Anastasia's almost-eleven-year-old heart, she didn't like them at all. Not one bit.

Anastasia shoved Viola Snodgrass's calling card into her pocket. Why did Miss Viola collect newspaper articles about missing children? She had been at the fair near Linus Shoetree right before he went missing. In the photograph, it looked like she was staring straight at him.

Perhaps she was some kind of Victorian private eye. That would explain the eyeball symbol. Viola Snodgrass: Watcher Extraordinaire. Were the Watchers a detective agency? Did they search for missing children?

But why would her aunties have the same silver ring? Had they been private eyes once upon a time? Was Miss Sneed an undercover Watcher, masking her concern for the students at Mooselick Elementary School behind a frightening monobrow?

If so, she was a terrific actress.

Perhaps all correct Victorian ladies documented their interest in the welfare of missing children. Perhaps the clippings had nothing to do with the Watchers. It was possible that the Watchers were simply a club of folks dedicated to, for example, bird-watching. Her aunties certainly loved bird-watching. Was it possible that Miss Sneed went in pursuit of blue-tootsied screech owls on her days off from terrorizing children?

But that brought Anastasia back to the mystery of Miss Sneed's portrait in the asylum. No, she thought, there was something more to the eyeball rings than an association of bird enthusiasts.

Anastasia jammed her sketch pad back into her satchel. Then she crawled up on her cot, her arms still rubbery from pulling the dumbwaiter.

Eeeeeeeeooooooooo.

She shifted, trying to get comfortable on the lumpy mattress.

OoooOooooooooooo.

Anastasia had Viola Snodgrass's calling card, but she still wasn't any closer to finding the source of the eerie yowling.

"It sounds," she informed Mr. Bunster, "like a ghost singing a lullaby."

Eeeooooo.

"A lullaby to its *ghost* children."

Mr. Bunster regarded her blankly.

Anastasia sighed. "Maybe I just have missing children on the brain." She wriggled deeper into the child-shaped hollow and shivered herself to sleep.

Anastasia's hunch that one of the portrait-sitters had lived in the asylum proved, as you have seen, correct. What other clues might she find in the sealed-off wings of the mansion? And where, oh where was Room Thirteen? The following day, she crawled through the little fairy door of Room Nine and let the asylum swallow her down into its secret innards, down to the story below. She pushed the door open a crack and peered out into a large room with huge wooden tables and a monstrous old stove. Long silver knives dangled from the ceiling like stalactites in a cave.

The kitchen. Anastasia's tummy let out a wail.

She looked left. She looked right. And then, like a brave mouse scurrying from its hole in the baseboard to forage for crumbs, Anastasia crept from the dumbwaiter, tiptoed across the floor, and started flinging the cupboards open.

Reader, perhaps your nanny or your mother or your father or a kind elementary school librarian like Miss Apple has recited for you the following beloved nursery rhyme:

Old Mother Hubbard went to the cupboard to fetch her
poor dog a bone.
But when she got there, the cupboard was bare—and so
the poor dog had none.

Why is this rhyme beloved, you might ask? What sort of sadist enjoys hearing about a Labradoodle deprived of its well-deserved snack? I can't answer your excellent questions, but I can confirm that Anastasia knew this little ditty by heart, and it trickled into her mind as she peered into the cabinets of the kitchen at St. Agony's Asylum.

To be accurate, the cupboards weren't completely bare. They were jumbled with copper jelly molds shaped like fish and roosters and enormous seashells. There was even a mold shaped like the asylum. There were canisters of flour and sugar and tea, but these were of little help to an almost-eleven-year-old girl who could barely toast bread without starting a fire. Anastasia consoled herself by sticking her finger into a pot of Happy Forest Maple Syrup and licking it clean, thinking of happier times munching Fred McCrumpet's signature waffles.

Tingalingaling! A bell chimed from afar, and Anastasia's eyes flicked to the kitchen window. The Gardener! Digging away by a shaggy topiary that had perhaps been a splendid elephant but now looked more like a beatnik mammoth. Anastasia pressed her nose against the glass and watched as

he shoveled more and more mud out of the ground. Why would anyone choose such a miserable day to dig a hole? What about his delicate lungs?

Anastasia's lungs were not delicate. They were young and robust, and her breath puffed onto the window and silvered the glass. She leaned back, raising her arm to wipe the fog with her sleeve, but froze midair.

Her breath was crystallizing on the glass, forming whorls and swoops and arabesques of frost until a patch of ice rimed one corner of the pane.

Could the asylum really be *that* cold? She traced one of the spirals with her forefinger, and then scratched at the frost with her thumbnail. Little icy bits chipped from the glass.

She leaned forward and huffed onto the window again, and again the glittering cloud of her breath swirled into fine silvery lace. But this wasn't just the feathery curlicues Mother Nature inscribes upon our car windshields on wintry mornings.

Right before Anastasia's eyes, *the frost was swirling into a picture.*

So fine it might have been traced by the hand of a fairy silversmith, the image of an arrow crystallized on the glass. And it was pointing down.

Anastasia's gaze followed the arrow's point. The kitchen sink? She frowned for a moment at the dirty dishes piled there, and then jerked her eyes back to the window. All that remained were a few icy twinkles, and these melted before she could blink. Had the arrow been some trick of her overwrought imagination?

A magical arrow pointing to the kitchen sink, indeed. She mustered a chuckle. And then the chuckle dissolved behind her tonsils.

Could the arrow have been pointing to something lower than the kitchen sink, even lower than the grimy floor?

Had it been pointing to the Forbidden Basement?

Anastasia whirled toward the dumbwaiter and saw for

the first time the peculiarities dangling from the wall by its door. It was a row of rubber tubes, and at the end of each of these tubes flared a silver funnel similar to the bell of a trumpet. Anastasia stood on her tippy-toes to read the little plates screwed to the wall above each hose.

MAIN PARLOR

BILLIARDS ROOM

WATCHTOWER

CONSERVATORY

Anastasia scrunched her eyebrows.

The tiniest of whispers—like a snake confessing its deepest secrets to its wise and pricey psychiatrist—hissed from the funnel attached to the Watchtower tube. With all the caution of a veteran herpetologist, Anastasia stretched out her hand and grasped the tube and lifted its tarnished bell to her ear.

Gentle Reader, have you ever created your own telephone with two tin cans connected by a length of string? If not, I advise you to do so. The sound of your friend's voice humming up the cord and jangling the tin can pressed to your ear will delight and amaze you!

Certain homes of yore were equipped with an in-house speaking system that operated on the same principles of the tin-can phone. A rubber hose snaking through the walls of the house connected two metal bells in separate rooms. With these speaking tubes, people in enormous houses (or lunatic asylums) could communicate without running themselves silly. The lady of the manor could call from her parlor down to the kitchen and request a figgy pudding, or a chocolate laxative bar, or whatever her heart desired.

The device to which Anastasia now pressed her ear, and through which whispered a voice from high above in one of the asylum's towers, was one of these speaking tubes.

"What do you think about her?" The voice was far, far away, but Anastasia recognized it at once. Auntie Prim! Her aunties' favorite birding post, Anastasia pondered, must have been used as a watchtower back in St. Agony's loony-bin days.

"She doesn't show much *potential*," replied Prude. "We've had her here for over a month, and I haven't seen anything to indicate she's different from any of the millions of brats that clog this earth. No potential there, I think."

"You never know how children will turn out," Prim said. "But she does seem rather a dreary little thing, doesn't she? Always moping about, telling boring stories about that ridiculous vacuum peddler. I've caught her crying once or twice." A high little giggle snaked its way through the tube and licked Anastasia's eardrum.

Her jaw dropped. They were talking about *her*!

"The necklace doesn't seem to be having any effect on her," Prude said. "I checked yesterday. Nothing."

"Still," Prim said, "we don't know everything about that beastly girl. We'll have to wait and see what happens."

Tears scorched Anastasia's eyes. *Dreary little thing? Beastly?* That's how her aunties really saw her? Anastasia was not, as you will remember, particularly fond of her aunties, but it was nonetheless hurtful to consider that Prim and Prude might dislike *her*. And did they really think she would forget her dead parents and orphaned guinea pig just because they gave her a stupid piece of jewelry?

Anastasia removed the silver bell from her ear and gazed at it, wondering whether the speaking tube could transmit things other than sound. Well, perhaps she would find out. She applied the bell to the seat of her pants. She grimaced.

After a moment, she returned the bell to her ear.

"Good Lord, Prudence, what is that ghastly odor?" Prim gasped.

"Primrose, was that *you*?"

"Certainly not!"

Retching noises jangled down the speaking tube.

Anastasia dropped the silver funnel and did a little jig right there in the kitchen, delighted at the success of her smellophone experiment. Beastly girl, indeed!

Rebellion swelling her almost-eleven-year-old heart, she climbed back into the dumbwaiter and pulled the door shut and rode down, down, down, all the way to the very bottom of the shaft, where she thumped to a stop.

She pushed the doors open into a dark hallway. Something trembled deep in Anastasia's core—something almost like a premonition of doom—as she hopped from the dumbwaiter into the darkness, clutching her candlestick.

She was in the Forbidden Basement.

❧ 13 ❧
The Ring of Mirrors

HER GALOSHES SQUEAKED like frightened mice against the tiled floors. The doors lining the hallway were very, very tall, and every single one had a little barred window near its top. Anastasia stood on her tippy-toes but, being an average height for an almost-eleven-year-old, remained many inches too short to see through the grimy glass.

She took a deep breath and opened the door.

"Waffle crumbs!"

The walls were upholstered from floor to ceiling in plushy fabric, like a couch or armchair. The floor was padded, too. After a few wobbly steps, Anastasia jumped up and down, hoping the cushioned floor would prove as springy as her little mattress back in the McCrumpet house. Her galoshes just sank into the padding, puffing up clouds of dust.

The other doors opened into similar padded cells. Anastasia peeked into all of them, and then she came to the end of the hallway, to a door without a window at its top. A plaque bolted to the heavy wood read: TREATMENT ROOM: CURES AND PUNISHMENTS.

Punishments? It gave Anastasia the heebie-jeebies, but she tested the knob and found that it twisted easily.

Her gaze hiccuped from shelves jumbled with glass bottles to the walls spangled with hungry-looking knives and saws and drills and needles. As would be the instinct of any sensible person, Anastasia wanted to sprint howling from this bizarre torture chamber. However, as she remembered from Francie Dewdrop's experiences, forbidden rooms often yielded the crème de la crème of clues. So she steeled her will and inched forward to plunder the first of many drawers lining the counter beneath the shelves.

Inside lay an enormous magnet of the variety you may have seen in cartoons: a red U with metal tips. Anastasia nabbed the magnet at its bend and aimed the ends at a pair of small scissors dangling from the collection of fearsome surgical equipment. *Th*-WHACK-*clink!* The scissors leapt from the wall and attached themselves to the magnet like a leech. Anastasia regarded the powerful magnet in admiration, then returned both it and the scissors to their respective places.

The other drawers yawned open like empty mouths,

and the cabinets beneath the counter were bare as those of Old Mother Hubbard, with one surprising exception. When Anastasia tugged the handle of the very last cupboard, it vomited forth a cascade of mangy teddy bears and limp-limbed dolls and fraying jump ropes and all sorts of other toys. Anastasia sorted through the mess in great puzzlement. Why would there be a *toy* cabinet in this frightening room?

Some of the toys were very old, and others quite new—in fact, there was a Francie Dewdrop title published about two years earlier, Mystery #63: *The Clue in the Hidden Room.* Anastasia hugged it to her chest, remembering the day back in third grade when Miss Apple had waved her into the library with a smile. "I saved this especially for you," the good librarian said, "so that you could be the first at Mooselick Elementary to read it."

Anastasia flipped the cover. *"Property of Lucy P.,"* she read, studying the bubbly cursive looping across the title page. "Well, Lucy P., I hope you don't mind if I borrow this." She shoved the book into her satchel, giddy with the anticipation of perusing a Francie Dewdrop by candlelight in Room Eleven that night.

Had Lucy P. lived in St. Agony's? Anastasia wondered how long the ancient nuthouse had been in her aunties' possession. They had never mentioned exactly *when* they'd become the proud owners of an authentically creepy Victorian asylum.

Leaning against the cabinet to squish the toys back inside, she spotted a door at the rear of the Treatment Room. She nipped through to another gloomy corridor. The doorknobs lining the darkness winked like bulbous eyes in the flicker from her candle. Anastasia paused by the first door on the left.

OFFICE OF DR. JASPER GRUNGEWHIFF

(THAT IS TO SAY:

ROOM FOR DIAGNOSING PSYCHOPATHIC MURDERERS,

DILLY ARSONISTS, LOONY PICKPOCKETS,

AND OTHER CRIMINAL FRUITCAKES)

A sturdy bolt glinted on the jamb. Why would there be a bolt on the *outside* of Dr. Grungewhiff's office?

Ding bling ting ting bing.

Was that *music* coming from the depths of Dr. Grungewhiff's lair? Anastasia plastered her ear to the door. *Bling ting tinkle tinkle bling.* She took a deep breath, then slid the rod back and gumshoed into the office.

Flames sputtered at the tops of dozens of candelabra scattered across the floor, throwing peculiar shadows over the walls. A ring of silver mirrors lay on the moldering carpet, and in the center of the circle lay a heap of clothing and a set of bellows. Beside the bellows glittered a small crystal box trimmed in gold.

Ding ting plinkle dinkle. A quirked crank whirred in the box's side. *Tinkle . . . ding . . . bling.* The crank slowed, then stopped. So did the music.

"Hello?" Anastasia whispered. "Is anyone here?"

But the room was completely empty.

How was it possible? She had just come through the only entry, and it had been locked from the outside. And why were candles lit down here? Was this, perhaps, *the Gardener's room*? She hopped over the moat of mirrors and stooped to peer through the box's glass flanks at its gilded guts. She twirled the crank. *Ding ting dinkle . . .*

It was, Anastasia realized with a shock, *the ghostly melody. Plink.*

Two brown lace-up shoes lay on their sides near the jumble of clothing. She inserted her pinkie finger into the crisscross of laces, lifted one brogue to her nostrils, and sniffed.

"It smells," she whispered, *"like boys' feet."*

Swamped with shivers, she dropped the shoe and staggered out of the circle of mirrors. Her stomach twisted. Maybe it was another premonition of doom (they were getting quite frequent, these premonitions!), or maybe it was all the Happy Forest Maple Syrup she had gobbled in the kitchen. Either way, she let loose with a ripping flabbergaster.

"Teeheeheeheehee!"

Anastasia gasped. "Who's there?" She leapt to the door and scanned the corridor. It was empty.

She let out a shaky breath. Perhaps there was a speaking tube somewhere in the basement and one of her aunties' giggles had jangled down from the Watchtower. Anastasia slunk back into the mirrored room. Her gaze drifted from the cobwebs clogging the corners to her shadows twitching on the walls. They all bowed in unison as she crouched to retrieve her candlestick.

All except one.

One shadow remained standing upright.

A big lump formed in Anastasia's throat. Was it a stain on the wallpaper? A *child-shaped* stain? She crept forward and touched the shadowy figure with the very tip of her index finger.

"Teeheehee!" The dark form slithered from beneath her hand and darted across the wall.

Anastasia recoiled, tripping over her galoshes.

"Wait!" cried a little voice. "Wait! Please! Don't go!"

You can imagine some of the concerns that flooded Anastasia's cranium. Was St. Agony's Asylum driving her as barmy as one of its insane Victorian inmates? Was she imagining voices, or had the shadow actually *spoken*? *Was the thing on the wall a ghost?*

"Don't leave yet," piped the little voice. "We haven't even met properly."

❧ 14 ❧

Pink Footprints

EVEN THOUGH ANASTASIA'S head twizzled with all variety of frightful fancies as she hurdled from the chamber, she had the wits to slam the door shut and latch it. Then she fled the Forbidden Basement, heaving herself back up the dumbwaiter shaft as fast as her arms would haul her. She tore through the asylum higgledy-piggledy-willy-nilly, all the way back to Room Eleven.

Panting, she leaned against the doorjamb, staring down at her reflection blurred in the mirror bolted to the carpet. Did she *look* crazy? Could one tell just by looking? She squinched her eyes shut and conjured up a phantasm of the Gardener. *He* seemed loopy from the first glance. Of course, anyone who went around with a birdcage on his head would.

She blinked and refocused her eyes. *Something was written in the dust fuzzing the mirror's blotchy cheek.*

Anastasia squatted and dug in her pocket for a match. Her candle had wheezed out in her mad dash, and she fumbled to light it again. She peered at the letters gleaming against the grime.

NEED TO TALK ROOM 38 DANGER

Anastasia uncorked her memory, and a faraway murmur rustled her mind's ear: *We need to talk.* The Gardener! *He* must have traced this mysterious message. Her aunties certainly hadn't crouched here to send her a secret warning. *Danger?* But wasn't the Gardener dangerous himself? He was a lunatic biter!

Lunatic biter. That's what her aunties had told her. And her aunties had called *her* a beast and a dreadful girl and all sorts of things. If they thought that about a perfectly pleasant almost-eleven-year-old, maybe they had fudged their tales about the Gardener, too.

DANGER. The letters wiggled and twitched in the candlelight like silvery centipedes. Did the Gardener, perhaps, know about the ghost in the basement? Her thoughts unspooled to the day she had seen him creeping around the hallway, flattened against the walls as though he didn't want to be seen. Maybe he was frightened of something. A prickle tiptoed up Anastasia's spine, and she slowly swiveled her head over her shoulder.

Prim was standing behind her. Something long and sharp glinted in her raised hand. Even though Prim was a teeny tiny old lady, she looked huge from where Anastasia hunkered among the dust bunnies. Her mouth was slightly open, and her pointy metal teeth glistened in the gloom.

"Oh!" Anastasia cried. "I didn't hear you, Auntie!"

Prim lurched, and the thing in her hand fell to the floor with a harmless tinkle. It was, Anastasia saw, just a knitting needle.

"Now look what you made me do," Prim chided, stooping to pick it up. "Ouch! My poor knees!" She slipped the needle into her coat pocket. "You shouldn't be playing on the floor. Haven't you noticed all the poison ivy creeping around this place?"

Anastasia fumbled to cover the cryptic mirror memo. "There isn't any ivy growing in here, Auntie."

"The last thing we need is a rashy orphan on our hands," Prim went on. "Speaking of rashes, what are those spots on your neck?" She plucked at Anastasia's collar, inspecting the silver chain of Granny McCrumpet's necklace for just a second before snatching her hand away.

"Like I keep telling you," Anastasia said, "I'm just freckly."

"Well, poison ivy or not, you shouldn't be lollygagging,

dear. You're supposed to be helping your frail-hearted aunties with the housework," Prim said. "But no gardening today. It's too wet."

"I saw the Gardener outside," Anastasia said. "He was digging a hole in the garden. A *big* hole."

Prim fumbled in her purse. "It's for a rosebush," she said. "Prude and I so love our roses."

"I thought the Gardener had delicate lungs," Anastasia persisted.

"Where *are* my heart pills?" Prim mumbled. "I must have left them up in the tower." Her umbrella thumped as she wandered away.

How different Prim had looked looming in the hallway, metal dentures twinkling so strangely in the candlelight! It had almost seemed as if the old woman was baring her teeth. Anastasia shivered, marveling at the effects of St. Agony's Asylum on her nerves.

But her gaze hopscotched back to the message in the dust. *DANGER.* She wasn't imagining *that.* Room Thirty-Eight. Did she dare visit the Gardener? She longed for someone to talk to. She couldn't ask her aunties about the ghost in the cellar, because they would just say it was a product of her overactive imagination. And then they would scold her for exploring the Forbidden Basement.

Perhaps they would even lock her into her room.

Anastasia smeared her palm across the mirror, then

tottered to her feet and beelined to the stairwell. *DANGER.*
Her pulse thudded as she vaulted the steps. *DANGER.* She
burst into the hallway, the urge to bolt twitching her galoshes
from pussyfooting to cantering. *DANGER.* From cantering
to dashing. *DANGER! DANGER! DANGER!*

She wheezed to a halt, realizing that she had gotten all
muddled up in the hallways. A draft of icy air rattled down
the corridor and gnawed at her bones. Was she in the wintry
North Wing, where frostbite ravaged the toes of orphans?
As Anastasia whirled to turn back, her candlelight snagged
on something small and metallic glittering on the floor. She
knelt.

It was a key, and inscribed in silvery loops on its head was
a number, 13.

"Miss Viola's key!" Anastasia
whispered.

She scrutinized the carpet. Dust
veiled the rose-splotched runner, but
the pink showed through in a set of
footprints twisting down a crooked
hallway.

Anastasia pulled out her magnifying glass, squinting through it at
the crimson tracks as she trailed them
into the gloom. She was so focused
on the view through the magical lens,

in fact, that she smacked right into the wall at the end of the corridor. She toppled backward, rubbing her scalp. A dead end. Had there even been any doors along the way? She hadn't noticed. She scurried back up the passageway and confirmed: there wasn't a single doorway lining its walls. She returned to the cul-de-sac and peered at the peeling green wallpaper, perplexed.

It was a hallway to nowhere.

And yet—someone had *just* been there. The footprints were recent. St. Agony's was so grubby that she could spend an entire afternoon sweeping grime off the floor and awaken the following morning to find a new blanket of dust in its place, like snow that had fallen overnight. These tracks, she mused, must have been made that morning, or perhaps sometime after lunch. She lowered her candle, puddling light over the pink footprints. They seemed to walk right into the wall.

Anastasia stared at the not-door. She stared at it until she started to see faces in the botanical wallpaper print. Your imagination may have veneered similar faces over patterned wallpaper in your own home, or perhaps you have watched clouds in the sky transform into fluffy bunnies before your fanciful gaze. Anastasia giggled. The faces looked a bit like Prim and Prude: one skinny face (a pointy thistle); one round face (a squashed cabbage); one skinny face; one round face; one round face; one round face—

"Wait a minute," Anastasia whispered. She raised the magnifying glass to the cluster of printed cabbages. The wallpaper lumped and buckled, just a little. She could just make out a seam where someone had patched the paper. It blended almost perfectly with the rest of the wall, but who-ever gummed it up should have planted a thistle instead of another cabbage.

Of course, all the wallpaper in the house was torn and tattered and rotting away. But why, Anastasia wondered, had someone bothered to fix *this* wall, in a hallway that led to nowhere?

Crooking her thumb and forefinger, she peeled back the square of paper.

And there, like a little yawning golden mouth, gleamed a keyhole.

❦ 15 ❦

Peppermints

THE SILVER KEY said *click*. The tumblers tumbled.

Anastasia sidled into the room and shut the door behind her, her gaze swiveling from the crackling fireplace to two plump chairs angled by a coffee table. On the coffee table was a big silver tray set with tea things and, Anastasia saw (and smelled), *sweets*.

Her hunger yanked her across the plush rugs. There were two china cups on two china saucers. There was a tall teapot with steam curling from its nose. There was a little bowl of sugar cubes. There were pots for jam and other tasty treats. But best of all, there were plates heaped with frosted cakes and rolls dotted with raisins and sandwiches cut into triangles.

After weeks and weeks of Mystery Lumps and the

occasional moth, Anastasia did not stop to consider that perhaps one should not eat the forbidden cakes of secret rooms. She plunked down her candlestick and grabbed one of the cakes—piping hot; it must have just come out of the oven—and it was in her belly before she even had a chance to taste it. She took another cake, savoring the warmth seeping through her palms. She nibbled it as she strolled around Room Thirteen.

So this lovely little parlor had been Miss Viola's stomping grounds one hundred years earlier. It was, Anastasia thought, a very pleasant, very pretty room. The wood furniture gleamed with lemon-scented polish. On every shining surface of every tabletop and mantelpiece and shelf were photographs in frilly silver frames. She wondered why her aunties did not spend their days in this cozy nook instead of the drafty tower where they spied on red-ringed kookaburras and wimble-banded long-beaks. Room Thirteen offered a fine view of the woods. Of course, Prim and Prude had said there was no Room Thirteen in the asylum. Was it possible that they didn't know about the hidden parlor? No, she thought. They just wanted to keep this room to themselves. Maybe they thought she would break something.

Still munching the cake, she ambled over to a cluster of pictures on a dinky desk and picked one up.

It was a boy with bright blue eyes, about eleven years old, his glum face a bit blurry. Anastasia thought it was not a photograph worth displaying. She set it back down on the davenport, swallowed the last morsel of cake, and moseyed over to examine the pictures on the wall.

More photographs of children. Some of the pictures were in color, some were in black-and-white, and some were tinged brown. Some of them were obviously taken quite recently, and others looked about a hundred years old. However, all the pictures were similar in one aspect: every child was about ten or eleven or twelve years old. And Anastasia thought every child looked ill at ease, as though he or she were wearing wet socks or underpants that didn't quite fit, or had just had a tooth pulled.

Not a single one was smiling.

Anastasia frowned, too, wondering why her aunties collected photographs of unhappy children. What a peculiar and

unpleasant hobby. It reminded her of the grisly newspaper clippings in Miss Viola's Memories book.

She paused by a credenza glistening with polish. A large jar sat on the credenza, and in the jar was a jumble of peppermint candies. Anastasia wrinkled her nose, remembering the linty taste of the peppermint dredged from Auntie Prude's purse, so very many rainy weeks ago. The day, in fact, of her premonition of doom.

Next to the jar lay a tiny blue bottle and a little paintbrush, and one peppermint rested on the edge of a saucer. Anastasia picked up the bottle and read the label: DR. BLUSTER'S PATENTED SLEEP PREPARATION OF MOST SLEEPFUL SLEEP. "JUST ONE DROP WOULD KNOCK A RHINOCEROS ON ITS RUMP!"

Sleep preparation? She unstopped the bottle and snuffled its rim. No smell. Her eyes twitched from the sleep preparation to the paintbrush to the peppermint. Sleep preparation . . . paintbrush . . . peppermint.

She thought again of the peppermint lump in Auntie Prude's purse.

A spoonful of sugar helps the medicine go down.

Sleep preparation . . . paintbrush . . . peppermint.

"JUST ONE DROP WOULD KNOCK A RHINOCEROS ON ITS RUMP!"

How quickly had she conked out in the backseat of the pink station wagon? They hadn't been very far out of Mooselick.

Anastasia scrunched her eyebrows together. In fact, they had only been on the highway for about half an hour before she fell fast asleep. Why had she dozed off at nine o'clock in the morning? And now that she really thought about it, she had snoozed all day; when she awoke, it had been dark.

An unpleasant idea tugged at the edges of Anastasia's mind. She crossed the room again slowly, the somber faces of children blurring the sides of her vision until her gaze fixed on a photograph of a boy in a sailor suit.

Linus Shoetree.

All the pleasure of discovering Room Thirteen and being warm and gobbling sugared goodies evaporated. She bounded to the photograph and seized it off the whatnot. Her breath puffed out in an anxious gust, riming the glass with swirls and whorls. A silvery form crystallized beside Linus: *the silhouette of a woman wearing an enormous veiled hat.*

Anastasia gawped at the photograph in mute terror. The ice crystals twinkled beneath her gaze, then dissolved. She twisted to look at the picture displayed beside Linus's. She froze.

"Mr. Bunster?"

But this picture was from a day when Mr. Bunster still had both his eyes. His coat was clean and white; his ears, perky and pink. He was clutched in the hands of a pigtailed girl with rheumy eyes.

Thud. Thud. Thud.

She stiffened.

Footsteps.

Of course—the silver tray had been set out with the teapot still steaming, the cakes still fresh and warm. It was teatime in the secret parlor, and Anastasia had company.

❧ 16 ❧

Shadows in the Parlor

QUICKETY QUICK, ANASTASIA grabbed her candlestick off the table, snuffing out the flame with a gasp, and slipped behind one of the thick curtains draping the window. She hoped that the teatimers would not notice the lump of her fur-swaddled form beneath the green velvet. She pressed against the pane, trying to make herself as small as possible.

"Not only did you lose the key, you left the door unlocked!" complained a high, thin voice. Auntie Primrose! Anastasia shrank even farther into her coat.

"You're so careless, Prude," Prim sniped.

"Oh, poo," Prude replied. "Nobody would ever find that door."

"Perhaps not," Prim said, "but an ounce of prevention

is worth a pound of cure. Particularly when the cure," she added, "is so very, very nasty."

"Don't these cakes smell good!" cried Prude. "I'm famished!"

Mean old bags! Anastasia brooded. They'd been saving all the teensy tea sandwiches and muffins and sweets for themselves, while she suffered through bowl after bowl of Mystery Lumps!

"I do wish we could have a proper tea more often," Prude said.

"Economy, my sister," Prim chided. "We've sunk a small fortune into silver, you know."

"This house is practically a silver mine," Prude replied. "Silver *everywhere.*"

"Your *mouth* is a silver mine." Prim chuckled. "Besides, we must be cautious. It wouldn't do to neglect our watching, and the view from this room isn't as good as the one from our tower."

Anastasia held her breath on the other side of the curtain, not exactly sure why she was hiding but feeling quite positive that she should remain hidden. Obviously her aunties didn't want anyone else coming into their special Room Thirteen. They'd even hidden the keyhole.

Did the aunties lock themselves in this secret room so they could devour their lovely tea delicacies without sharing a single bite? Or might the aunties' secrecy have something to do with the dreary photographs of children?

Knitting needles began to click.

"Like I said, we must be more cautious," Prim said. "We must beware of *it*." The word *it* hissed a little between her metal teeth.

"It simply makes my skin crawl," Prude said. "I can barely stand being so close to it."

"Neither can I," Prim murmured. "Why, my skin is crawling right now just thinking about it."

"Knowing it's nearby, even when we can't see it," Prude went on. "Knowing that beastly creature could come for us at any minute."

Creature? Anastasia's eyes widened. What creature? Were they talking about the ghost in the basement? She shifted behind the drape. There was a little rip in the velvet, the perfect size for a peephole, and Anastasia peeped into Room Thirteen. Long shadows crawled across the room. Her aunties were sitting in the squishy chairs, their knitting needles flashing, their chins bearded with teatime jam.

"You must put on a brave face, Prudence," Prim said. "It can *smell* fear, you know. It thrives on it! You must never show your fear."

"It's the waiting that vexes me," Prude quavered.

"I know exactly what you mean," Prim said. She sighed and shook her curly pink head. "Still, that's our duty—watch and wait."

"Watch and wait," Prude repeated darkly. "Watch and wait."

Prim muttered, "By the pricking of my thumbs . . ."

"Something wicked this way comes," Prude chorused.

"That's always been my favorite line of poetry," Prim said. "So sad and so true. There's so much wickedness in this world. Why, it's all around us."

Her cloudy eyes lifted from her knitting to a window with its curtains drawn. Her gaze lingered on the trees in the distance before shifting back into the parlor, across the silver-framed photographs twinkling in the firelight. "So much evil," she murmured.

Anastasia's forehead tingled. For what wicked creature were they watching and waiting, exactly? It certainly wasn't a red-speckled twit. And it didn't seem like her aunties were talking about a ghost bolted into a basement room.

She thought of Prim's hands trembling as she stared through the bars of the iron fence and declared that they mustn't stay out after dark. She thought of her aunties stationed in the Watchtower, gazing through their binoculars as the poodles patrolled the gardens.

She thought of the way her aunties always locked her door at night.

"Primmy, dear," Prude said, "pass me another one of those scrumptious lychees."

Prim set her knitting in her lap, then took the lid off one of the little china bowls and pulled out something long and black and twitching. Whatever it was, it was certainly not a lychee fruit.

"Mmm." Prude plucked it from her sister's fingers and popped it into her mouth. Her metal teeth gnashed. Crimson dribbled down her chin. "Delicious!"

Prim also helped herself to one of the squirmy black delicacies. "And packed with all sorts of vitamins."

Prude stretched her arm toward the china bowl again.

"Leeches are like potato chips," she sighed. "You can never have just one."

Anastasia had to bite her lips to keep the screams from pouring out. *Leeches!* Not lychees! And the red stuff oozing down her aunties' jowls wasn't *jam*! It was—

"The sun is setting," Prim said. "We should go find the girl soon."

Trapped between the curtain and the window, Anastasia turned her head and watched the sun sink behind the thorny Dread Woods. She wondered whether, deep in the forest, the fearful creature was beginning to stir. Her heart thumped.

"Do you suppose," Prude asked, "that she suspects anything?"

Anastasia suppressed a yelp.

"Suspect anything?" Prim paused. "Oh, I shouldn't think so. Most children are rather stupid, you know. Beastly little dreadfuls."

"The last one started getting skittish toward the end," Prude said. "It seems there are never enough moppets to satisfy—"

"Hush," Prim chided. "Don't start talking that way. What would Auntie Vy think? Why, she'd spin in her grave to hear you carrying on so!"

Auntie Vy! Was she talking about *Viola Snodgrass*?

"But, Primmy," Prude bleated, "sometimes I feel so *tired*. Think of all the little hearts we've handed over. Not that I feel bad for those brats, of course, but I hate touching their slippery tickers."

"We'll have another one soon enough, I think," Prim said. Then she recited, *"Mary, Mary, quite contrary, how does your garden grow?"*

"With silver bells and cockleshells and little bones all in a row!" Prude replied in a singsong.

The breath Anastasia had been holding all this time whooshed out of her lungs and onto the windowpane. Tiny ice crystals swirled and swooped into an *R,* then a *U,* and an *N,* until the frost had curled across the glass to spell out an entire message in perfect birthday-cake cursive:

There are many ways to cope with nerves.

You can nibble your fingernails.

You can crawl beneath your quilts.

When Anastasia was nervous or worried, she itched to crawl into someplace cozy and quiet and have a think. Back in the McCrumpet house, this place had been her closet, cushy with mangy stuffed animals and outgrown sweaters and her rolled-up sleeping bag. It wasn't that she was an unusually fretful child. She wasn't. However, everyone has problems and needs to go away to think from time to time.

At St. Agony's Asylum, Anastasia had plenty to worry about. (Leech-gobbling aunties! The hideous creature lurking in the woods! A ghost in the basement! And so forth!) But she didn't have a closet in which to worry about them. She did, however, have a creepy wardrobe stuffed full of musty coats, and you would perhaps be surprised by just how snug a creepy wardrobe can be. It was into this wardrobe that Anastasia scrambled after fleeing Room Thirteen.

She scrunched into the fur coats. Tears drizzled down her dirty cheeks.

"Mr. Bunster," she whispered, "what is the thing in the woods? And why are Prim and Prude feeding it children's hearts? Are their gardens really full of bones?"

Mr. Bunster remained mum.

"And what did they mean, *the last one*?" She peered out of the wardrobe at the child-sized dust angel squashed into the mattress of her cot. Then she slid the picture of Mr. Bunster's rightful owner from the inside of her coat. She turned the frame over and pried out the photograph.

Something was written on the back in squiggly old lady script, the letters squished together like smashed spiders. She squinted.

What in the name of holy hopscotch did *that* mean?

"Was Lucy the last one?" Anastasia whispered to Mr. Bunster. "The last one to go . . . to go *to the DREADFUL?* What's the Dreadful? The Dread Woods?"

She chewed on the end of one of her braids, wondering about the creature in the black thorny wilderness beyond the iron bars. He munched the hearts of children. Could he be a bear? A wolf? Prude was always worried about wolves. Was it the ghost in the basement? Did the ghost go wandering from its mirrored room into the dark and dismal forest? Anastasia frowned. The ghost had giggled and then, in a high little voice, begged her not to leave. The high little cry of a child, she mused. Was it the ghost of one of the children? The basement phantom was not, she thought, the Creature.

"Oh, Mr. Bunster," she mumbled. "Who was Lucy P—"

Her breath rasped against her tonsils, and she dug in her satchel for the Francie Dewdrop book pilfered from the Treatment Room. She peeled back the cover so fast that it nearly tore clean from the binding.

Property of Lucy P.

Lucy Pinkerton!

Had Lucy Pinkerton been in the Treatment Room?

And what about all the other toys stashed in the hideous cellar room? Had the whirligigs and whatnot belonged to all the children whose portraits adorned the secret parlor?

"Linus Shoetree," she muttered. Viola Snodgrass's silhouette had crystallized on the glass beside him. It was just like the photograph at the fair. "It was right before she snatched him," Anastasia deduced. "*That's* why she was hovering nearby. She waited until he ran off to buy cotton candy and she kidnapped him." A terrible shiver coursed down her spine. The Watchers wasn't an organization that hunted for missing children. The Watchers was an organization that *snatched* them!

And her aunties were members. The evil Watcher eyeball winked from their pinkies. They were *watching and waiting,* and they certainly weren't talking about looking at birds. And *were* they even her aunties? Did the Watcher women work together to feed little hearts to the Creature in the Woods, whatever it was? Had Prim and Prude swooped in to kidnap her when they heard about the McCrumpets' freak vacuum accident? Perhaps the nefarious Miss Sneed had telephoned to inform them about the wonderful opportunity to snatch a valuable orphan.

"Anastasia?"

It was Prude. The door to Room Eleven creaked as the old woman pulled it open a crack.

Anastasia's throat closed like a fist.

"Anastasia?"

"I—I'm in here," Anastasia stammered. "I'm sleepy."

"All right, moppet. Good night."

The key clunked in the lock and the chain scraped across the door.

Anastasia burrowed deeper into the wardrobe. The fur coats were warm around her. Finally she drowsed off, cheeks still damp with tears, half dreaming that she could feel heartbeats thudding in the fur coats that cuddled her.

Suddenly her own heartbeat jozzled her awake, walloping her ribs and jiggling her tonsils. *What if her parents had never had an accident?*

Perhaps it had all been a lie to trick her into the pink station wagon!

Could Mr. and Mrs. McCrumpet be alive?

❧ 17 ❧
Strange Notes

IT IS AT exactly this point in our story that Anastasia's number one priority switched from cultivating her detective skills to plotting her escape from St. Agony's Asylum. That is, she was going to RUN FOR HER LIFE. It wouldn't be easy. Even if she somehow managed to successfully sneak past her aunties' watchful eyes, and evade the fearsome pack of guard poodles, and scale the spiky electric fence—where would she go? St. Agony's sat atop a hill in the middle of the Dread Woods. And somewhere in those woods lurked . . . the *Creature*.

Even as the impossibility of escape loomed before her, Anastasia knew that she had to try. She would not just sit back and wait to be crunched like a potato chip.

As you launch a daunting and complicated task, some

well-intentioned person may advise you that *the best way to eat an elephant is one bite at a time.* It isn't a particularly nice saying (elephants are such lovely creatures, and it breaks my heart to imagine one coming to harm!), but there is, nonetheless, wisdom embedded in these rather unpleasant words. If you have a big job ahead of you, the best way to set to work is by breaking it into smaller, more manageable chores. Anastasia decided that, before she worried about the endless hurdles awaiting her outside St. Agony's Asylum, she would solve the first problem within it—the chained and locked door to Room Eleven.

Now, Anastasia had journeyed to St. Agony's on short notice. She had not had an opportunity to pack a toothbrush or an extra pair of underwear or to hover over her suitcase, pondering, "Should I take my swimming suit? The light or heavy sweater? Will I wind up trapped in an authentic Victorian insane asylum? Shall I pack an ax, just in case I need to chop my way out of my room?"

Nope. She was unprepared. She would have to make do with what she had.

Unfortunately, Reader, this is the way lots of things in life go.

Early the next morning, Anastasia examined the safety pin that had fastened her Halloween flying squirrel tail to the seat of her jeans. She pinched it open. In Mystery #66: *The Ghostly Bell Tower,* Francie Dewdrop jimmied a lock with nothing but a hairpin and brainpower. Anastasia crouched by the keyhole to Room Eleven. She bent the sharp end of the safety pin back and poked it about in the lock. The pin wrestled against metal. A brassy crunch belched from the keyhole.

Success! Anastasia tumbled forward as the door swung open.

Prude smiled at her. "You're up early!" she chirped. "But what on earth are you doing down there?"

Anastasia gaped up at the old kidnapper. "I—I'm practicing yoga," she finally stammered.

"I've never understood the benefit of contorting oneself like some kind of demented octopus," Prude said. "It seems rather unhealthy to me. If you want some good exercise, moppet, there's plenty of sweeping to be done." She turned and plodded off.

Anastasia glared at the crumpled safety pin in her palm. She hadn't picked the lock—Prude had just opened the door with her key! She flung the pin to the floor and followed Prude down to breakfast, her mind percolating with ways to escape St. Agony's Asylum and get back to Mooselick and— hopefully!—her parents.

After swallowing her last Mystery Lump, Anastasia scooted from the breakfast table. She had a busy morning ahead of her. For one, she needed to borrow something from the Treatment Room. (In this paragraph, the word *borrow* is a polite way to say *pilfer*. And *pilfer* is a quaint synonym for *steal*.) As you will remember, the Treatment Room contained a delightful assortment of diabolical metal instruments for sawing, poking, stabbing, and pinching. There was also a magnificent magnet tucked into one of the drawers. This magnet, Anastasia reasoned, could be of help in her escape. Can you, alert Reader, guess how?

However, before she ventured down to the Forbidden Basement, Anastasia had important business to conduct on the third floor. She wanted to talk to the Gardener. The prospect made her knees turn to jelly—what if he was still upset about the toe-squishing incident outside Room Twenty-Four? But the Gardener knew something about the danger in the asylum. He had tried to warn her. Perhaps he could reveal more about the Creature, or Prim and Prude.

EEEEEEEooooooooow.

The weird whale-singing melody!

Eeeeee . . . eeeeEEEEEEeeee . . .

Anastasia panted at the top of the stairwell. *Eee-aaooooo . . .* Her pulse knocked in her throat and wrists as she skedaddled through the shadows toward the ghostly wails, chasing the tune. *Eeeeeoooo.* Her candlelight wobbled in a mirror screwed into a doorway. Anastasia's breath whistled through her nostrils. *Room Thirty-Eight.*

The door was ajar. *EeeeeeOOOOOOeeeeee.*

Anastasia sidled over the mirror and into the room. The music stopped abruptly.

Tingalingaling.

She whirled around.

Licks of silver gleamed in the darkest corner of the dark little chamber. And then, from this lightless pocket, a gangly figure crept forth. Staring at the saw dangling from the Gardener's hand, Anastasia worried her visit had been a mistake.

Tingalingaling!

He lifted the blade.

Anastasia plastered herself against the moldering wallpaper, imagining her own epitaph: *Here lies Anastasia McCrumpet, average to goodish triangle player, sliced and diced by lunatic Gardener. YOU WILL BE MISSED, PERHAPS.*

However, to her great astonishment, the Gardener did *not* lunge forth to carve her down the middle. He swiped the bedraggled tails of his jacket aside and sat down on a spindly chair. He plucked a violin bow off the floor. He squeezed one end of the saw between his knees and clutched the other with his hand, and closed his eyes.

He swiped the bow across the saw.

Eeeeeeee . . . ooooooOOoooo . . . Awoohhhhhoooo . . .

He curved the blade to produce different pitches, coaxing a peculiar melody from the rusty metal. Anastasia stared at him in sheer wonderment. Now that she knew it wasn't

the chimneys of St. Agony shrieking, or a ghost crying, she thought the sound was simply lovely.

Eeeeeeooooo.

The violin bow dropped by his side.

"That was beautiful," Anastasia whispered.

"Thank you." The Gardener looked tremendously pleased. "It's called 'Ballad of the Love-lorn Beluga.'" The smile fizzled off his lips, and he set his saw and the violin bow on the floor. "But you're not here to discuss music. You got my warning. It was a giant risk, writing it out like that. Prim or Prude might have seen it. But you ran away when I tried to talk to you. And you threw a book about lobotomies on my toes." He paused. "I must say, that was rather unfriendly."

"I'm sorry," Anastasia said. "I didn't mean to! I was afraid of you."

"Afraid?" the Gardener cried. "Of *me*?"

"I mean," Anastasia faltered, "you work for them, and—"

"Work for them! You mean Prim and Prude?" the boy said. "You think I'm in on their awful tricks, like some kind of a—a henchman?"

"Not a *henchman*," Anastasia protested. "No, I'm sure you're a very nice gardener, and good at your job—"

"Gardener?" he exclaimed. "I'm not a gardener!"

"Then who are you?" Anastasia gulped. "What are you doing here?"

"My name is Quentin Drybread," the boy said. "But the question you should really be asking is: what are *you* doing here? Those two ladies did not invite you here for Christmas jollies. I broke out to warn you the night they brought you here, but Prim chased me off with her poisonous umbrella. You must run for your life, Anastasia McCrumpet."

Anastasia's voice stuck in her throat. "I know."

"I'll help you," Quentin said, gripping his birdcage. "I'll help you leave this vile madhouse."

"But what about you?" Anastasia asked. "If you hate the asylum so much—"

"I can't leave." Quentin slumped back onto the chair. "I can't leave yet."

"Why not?"

"I'm . . . I'm looking for something."

"Looking for something?" Anastasia echoed. "What?"

"Something they took from me," he said so quietly that she could barely hear him. "Something important. I can't leave until I find it."

That explained his Most Mysterious Behavior. Sort of. Anastasia's brain whirred. "Is it a pet hamster?"

"No."

"How about your watch? Is it a nice watch with all kinds of cogs and whirligigs spinning in the face? And," she added, scrunching her face in thought, "a luminescent dial?"

"No."

"Those are nice watches," she said wistfully.

"Yes, they are," he agreed. "But I do not own one of them. Look, I can't tell you what it is. It's—it's a secret."

"If you told me, then maybe I could help you find it," Anastasia offered.

"I doubt it," the boy said, his pale face miserable. "You're too little. I bet you're only ten years old."

"I am almost eleven," Anastasia retorted. An idea prickled her mind. "Is it a music box?"

"Music box?" Quentin's head jerked up, the birdcage bell tinkling. "Did you say *music box*?"

"I found one," Anastasia said. "And it plays 'Ballad of the Lovelorn Beluga.'"

Quentin stared at her. "Where is it?"

"Down in the basement," Anastasia said. "In a room full of mirrors. And there's a ghost, too." Her face went pink. "At least, I'm pretty sure it's a ghost. I thought it was a shadow at first. Whatever it is, it's . . . ticklish."

"Ticklish?" Quentin leapt up. "Take me there!"

"All right," Anastasia said. "I hope you don't mind dark, cramped places or creepy Forbidden Basements."

"I'm rather fond of both," Quentin replied. "But please, before we go, can you remove that mirror? I—I can't cross over mirrors."

"Why not?" Anastasia asked. "Is it some kind of superstition, like walking under a ladder?"

"Er—yes! Something like that. Do you have a screwdriver?"

"No." Anastasia scrutinized the bolts securing the mirror to the floor. Then she plucked a quarter from her satchel, pressed its edge into the notch at the top of the screw, and twisted. "Righty tighty," she muttered. "Lefty loosey. I saw my dad do this once, when he put a new license plate on our car."

"He sounds like a brilliant man," Quentin said.

"Pretty good at making waffles, too," Anastasia said, tears stinging her eyes as she wondered whether she'd ever taste a Fred McCrumpet breakfast again. She lefty-looseyed all the screws, and then shoved the mirror aside.

Down in the asylum dungeon, they hurried past the padded cells, through the Treatment Room, and back to Dr. Grungewhiff's office for diagnosing fruitcakes. Anastasia hesitated by the doorjamb, but Quentin dashed past her into the room. "Where is he?"

Anastasia crept in behind him. The flickering flames from the candelabra sent their shadows dancing around them in a ghostly conga line. "Well, it—*he*—was right there. But now he's gone."

"There!" Quentin muttered. "Up in the corner!"

Sure enough, a shadowy figure twitched against the crumbling plaster near the ceiling.

"Pudding!" the boy called. "It's me! Come down."

Anastasia goggled as the child-shape slid down the wallpaper until its shadow feet alighted on the baseboard.

"Anastasia," Quentin said, "this is—"

"Ahem." The shadow cleared its throat. "I'm—er—in my birthday suit, you know."

I'm sure you would expect Anastasia to let out a holler of pure fright at the sound of a talking shadow. At the very least, a premonition of doom might wring her tummy. However, nothing like this happened. At the first mention of birthday suit, Anastasia fled Dr. Grungewhiff's office and hid in the corridor, squeezing her eyes shut.

"All right, Anastasia," Quentin called out after a minute. "You can come back in and meet my brother, Ollie."

❊ 18 ❊

The Dark Gauntlet

AN ALMOST-ELEVENISH BOY stood next to Quentin, tugging at the collar of his blue sweater, his plump face pink.

"Say!" the boy said. "You're the girl who tickled me the other day!"

"I—I didn't mean to," Anastasia stuttered. "I thought you might be a stain on the wall."

"A stain on the wall!" the boy cried. "Well, how do you like that? A *stain*! At least," he added, "*I* don't go around letting off flabbergasters in other people's rooms."

"I didn't know there was anyone else around!" Anastasia yelped.

"Flabbergasters?" Quentin said, eyeing her.

"Never mind that," Anastasia said hastily.

"Why did you run away?" the boy asked. "I wanted to talk to you."

"I thought you were a ghost," Anastasia apologized.

"A ghost!" the boy said. "First a stain, and then a ghost. Shows what you know."

"Well," Anastasia said, "what *are* you, exactly?"

"Quentin and I are—"

"*Shhhhh!* Ollie, you can't talk about those things!" Quentin hissed. "You know those are top-secret secrets!"

"That's right," Ollie mumbled. "Top-secret. Sorry, Q.

Hey, you have a birdcage on your head!" He squinted up at his brother. "It looks quite nice. Very smart."

"*Nice?*" Quentin sputtered. "*Smart?* It's *silver,* you pudding!"

"Silver!" Ollie squeaked. "Well, that changes things! *Silver!* Why on earth are you going around wearing a silver birdcage?"

"It's not a birdcage! It's an authentic Victorian head cage for *lunatics,*" Quentin said. "Don't you see the collar and the padlock? Those old prunes locked it on me after feeding me drugged tea."

"Oh," Ollie said. "Well, Quentin, you shouldn't have accepted drugged tea in the first place. When the old prunes said, 'Would you care for a cup of tea with sleeping stuff in it, my boy?' you should have told them, 'No, thank you!'"

Quentin heaved a mighty sigh. "I didn't know it was drugged, Ollie."

"What were you doing drinking tea with Prim and Prude, anyway?"

"I came here looking for you!"

"Right!" Ollie said. "Because I'd been kidnapped! Yes, now it's all starting to make sense."

"What about your parents?" Anastasia asked. "Weren't they searching for Ollie, too?"

Quentin shook his head. "They were out of town. A letter came earlier that week saying that our grandma was sick.

I'm sure it was just a trick, but Nanny lives—er—far away and doesn't have a phone."

"Mom and Dad left us with the fussy old lady next door," Ollie complained. "Her furniture is covered in plastic, and she made us look at slides of her trips to Hawaii."

"*And* she's very absentminded," Quentin said. "When I came home from orchestra practice that afternoon, Mrs. Gullwinch didn't even realize Ollie was missing. I couldn't call Mom and Dad, so I went out on my own."

"How did they get you, Ollie?" Anastasia asked. "They told me they're my great-aunties."

"They didn't pretend to be my aunties," Ollie said. "Or my uncles, for that matter. They just said they had a lot of sweets at their house."

"Ollie!" Quentin cried. "You should never take candy from strangers!"

"Well, that's funny," Ollie huffed. "Coming from someone who goes around drinking drugged tea."

"And the first candy they gave you was a peppermint?" Anastasia guessed.

"Right-o!" Ollie said. "How did you know? Golly, you're a smart one. Anyway, they brought me here and fed me all kinds of cookies and cakes. It was jolly fun for a couple of days."

"They gave you cake?" Anastasia said. "They've never given *me* cake. In fact, they go into a *secret room* to eat cake."

"Perhaps they like me more than you," Ollie suggested.

"I'm pretty likable, don't you think? Anyway, one night I umbrated in my sleep—"

"*Oliver Dante Drybread!*" Quentin exclaimed. "You know we can't talk about that stuff with anyone!"

Ollie squirmed. "But she already knows that we can turn into shadows. That's what umbrating is," he explained to Anastasia.

She gasped. "Unbelievable! And—and you umbrate, too, Quentin?"

He shook his head sadly and pointed at the silver cage.

"Silver is bad for us," Ollie said. "It saps our strength and makes it hard to umbrate. But back at home, Quentin umbrates like a *champ*. He can even do shadow puppet shows!"

Boys who turn into shadows! If Anastasia hadn't spent the past days watching frost twinkle into pictures and discovering kidnapping schemes and wondering about ghosts and heart-crunching forest Creatures, the fantastical fact of Quentin and Ollie's existence might have driven her plain cuckoo. But all the weirdness in St. Agony's Asylum had limbered up her mind for shocking surprises.

"Anyway," Ollie went on, "one night I umbrated in my sleep. That happens sometimes, you know. I woke up to see Prim and Prude hovering over me, grinning with those horrible teeth—oh, it was frightening! They whooshed me up into those bellows, and then they squished me out in the middle of this circle of mirrors." He shivered. "And now they only bring cakes down once each morning."

"The brutes!" Quentin swore.

"What do mirrors have to do with anything?" Anastasia asked.

"We can't cross mirrors," Ollie said. "We have to piggyback on a—um—a normal person. That's how I escaped the ring of mirrors the other day. I piggybacked on you, Anastasia. But then you ran away and locked the door. Pretty mean, I thought."

"I already told you, I thought you were a ghost," Anastasia said. She stared at the looking-glass prison glinting on the floor. That explained all the mirrors scattered around the asylum, including the one crammed up the parlor chimney.

"Poor pudding," Quentin said, squeezing Ollie into a hug. "Didn't you hear my music? I wandered all over this asylum, playing 'Ballad of the Lovelorn Beluga' on a saw."

"Now that you mention it, I *did* hear music!" Ollie said. "But I just thought it was a talented owl!"

"Ollie!" Quentin elbowed him. "I was hoping you'd hear it and call out for me. I've been combing this wretched place for two months!"

"Two months? So your parents should be looking for you by now," Anastasia mused. "And they've probably called the police."

"Probably," Quentin said. "But I don't know if they'll look *here*. St. Agony's is pretty far away from Melancholy Falls. This place is in the middle of nowhere, really."

"How did you even get here?" Anastasia asked. "Did you drive? *Can* you drive? Maybe we could take the station wagon and get out of here."

"I'm not old enough to drive," Quentin said. "I—I came here as a shadow."

"Shadows can move super fast, and cold doesn't bother us," Ollie said. "The only problem is, once you get where you're going, you need some clothes. Otherwise"—he lowered his voice to a whisper—"you're stuck walking around in your birthday suit."

"So that's why you're wearing old-timey clothing," Anastasia said to Quentin. "I thought it was just part of Prim and Prude's authentic Victorian experience, having their Gardener wear stuff like that."

"Q's not a gardener," Ollie scoffed. "What gave you that idea?"

"Well, because Prim and Prude said so," Anastasia said. "I know it isn't true now. But why . . ." She stared at Quentin. "Why *were* you digging that hole in the garden?"

Quentin grasped the collar on his cage. "Oh, Anastasia, you were right! I'm no better than a common henchman!"

"I never called you a henchman!" Anastasia protested.

"Prim and Prude threatened to do horrible things to

Ollie if I refused to dig that hole," Quentin said. "It's for . . . it's for you."

"For *me*?"

"That's why I wrote that note to you in the dust. Once they sent me out to start digging, I knew I had to warn you," Quentin said. "Prim and Prude are horrible! They're murderers!"

"So you know about the Creature in the Woods!" Anastasia whispered.

"*The Creature in the Woods?*" Quentin and Ollie echoed.

"Prim and Prude kidnap children and feed their hearts to the Creature. And then they bury the bones in their garden."

Ollie grabbed his brother's hand. "Is that true, Q?"

"I thought Prim and Prude were . . . a different kind of kidnapper," Quentin said. "But I didn't know anything about a Creature in the Woods. Anastasia, how did you find all this out?"

"Detective work," Anastasia said. "I heard Prim and Prude talking about the Creature in their secret parlor. I hid behind a curtain and spied on them."

"Just like Francie Dewdrop!" Ollie said. "I *told* you she was smart, Q."

"And," Anastasia added, wrinkling her nose, "I saw them eating *leeches*!"

"Leeches!" Ollie cried.

"Prim and Prude made me wade around in the bog and

catch leeches. They said they were going to sell them to the doctors in the village." The horrible details came pouring out. "But then I saw them *munching* the leeches."

"They leeched me, too," Quentin muttered.

"They must be after vitamin S!" Ollie said. "Packed with vitamin S, our blood is. Antivenin, you know."

"*Ollie!*" Quentin said. "You're not supposed to talk about these things with outsiders!"

"But, Quentin," Ollie argued, "Anastasia isn't *really* an outsider, is she? She's stuck here, just like us. Don't you think we can tell her that vitamin S protects against Shadowbites?"

"Shadowbites!" Anastasia exclaimed.

Quentin groaned and flung his hands into the air.

Ollie turned to Anastasia and clicked his teeth. "Shadowbites are deadly poisonous. But someone with Shadowblood in their veins can take it."

"So you really *do* bite!" Anastasia said to Quentin.

"Only on special occasions," he protested.

"And that's why Prim and Prude eat leeches?" Anastasia cried. "They're after your vitamin S?" She paused. "But they leeched me, too. And I'm not . . . Well, what *are* you, exactly?"

Ollie wriggled. "We're—"

"Be quiet, you pudding!" Quentin hissed.

"I know that you umbrate," Anastasia pointed out. "And I *did* help you find Ollie. Shouldn't that count for something?"

Quentin looked down at his grimy fingernails. "Fine," he said. "But first, Anastasia, we must swear you to secrecy."

"I swear," she promised. "Cross my heart."

"There are dire consequences for those who blab," Quentin warned. "*Most* dire."

"Like what?"

"Even the consequences are secret," Ollie whispered.

"I'm good at keeping secrets," Anastasia said. "I never told Prim and Prude that I saw you sneaking around, Quentin. Even after you scared me in the hall."

"Thank you," Quentin said. "That was very noble. Now you have to pinkie-swear." He held out his hand.

As you are undoubtedly aware, dear Reader, pinkie-swearing is the most hallowed of all oaths. Treaties have been ratified, and wedding proposals accepted, and brave soldiers knighted, all with the sacred pinkie clinch. It is not an oath to undertake lightly, and Anastasia knew this full well as she solemnly crooked her pinkie around Quentin's.

"Ollie and I," Quentin said, "are Shadowfolk."

"There are lots of us out in the world," Ollie said, "and we have to keep our existence completely hush-hush."

"Why?"

"Because of people like Prim and Prude, for one," Ollie said. "Leeching Quentin for his Shadowblood! The monsters!"

"Have they been leeching you, too, Ollie?" Quentin asked.

"Nope," Ollie said. "They want me to stay strong. They're waiting for me to molt."

"Molt?" Anastasia echoed.

"Shed my Shadowsilk. Shadowchildren—"

"*Shadowsilk?*"

"Cripes, you interrupt a lot," Ollie said. "We Shadowchildren shed shadows for a few years, from about fifth grade until eighth." He dug in his pocket. "Here's a bit that scraped off my arm the other day."

He pushed a long black glove into Anastasia's palms. It was silky and shimmery and cool. Anastasia stared at it.

"So Prim and Prude want your shadow bits? But why?"

"Sometimes we slough off our whole Shadowskin—like a snake shedding."

Anastasia gulped. "Does it hurt?"

"It's sort of like peeling a sunburn," Ollie said. "Anyway, when we slough like that, someone else can wear the Shadowsilk."

"Like a suit," Quentin spoke up.

Ollie nodded. "Like footie pajamas."

"But Prim and Prude are taller than you," Anastasia said.

"Shadowsilk is elastic stuff." Ollie grabbed the silken glove back from her and tugged its edges. "See?"

"But why would Prim and Prude want to wear your old skin? That's disgusting!"

"Gosh, you're rude!" Ollie said. "I'll show you!" He clumped into a corner untouched by candlelight and stretched the gossamer down over his hair and then his eyebrows, and finally over his nose and mouth and chin. "*Louis the Sixteenth!* He was decapitated, you know."

"Pineapple upside-down cake crumbs!" Anastasia exclaimed. "It *does* look like someone chopped off your head!"

"Shadowsilk is terrific camouflage," Quentin said. "You blend right into the shadows. It's almost like being invisible."

Ollie peeled the Shadowsilk off his head, and it shrank back into a glove. "Here, Anastasia. Give it a whirl."

Anastasia pushed her hand into the dark gauntlet, gasping as her fingers disappeared into the darkness. If she strained her eyeballs, she could detect a hand-shaped silhouette moving against the gloom. But barely.

"A suit made of this silk would be extremely handy for a kidnapper," she said, looking significantly at Ollie and

Quentin. "They could sneak around and snatch children without even being seen!"

Quentin scowled. "Bingo."

"Oh, I *love* that game," Ollie said. "Do you play, Anastasia?"

"This is no time for games," Quentin said. "We have to figure out how to escape this lousy asylum. What do you think those kidnappers are going to do to you, Ollie, when they finally get their nice shadow suit?"

Ollie's eyes swiveled to the ceiling in deep thought. Then he solemnly drew his index finger across his neck. "Creature in the Woods?"

Quentin nodded. "Prim and Prude aren't keeping us around because they *like* children, after all. We've got to get out of here. We must escape—*or die trying.*"

❖ 19 ❖

The League of Beastly Dreadfuls

"ALL RIGHT," OLLIE said cheerfully. "Escape or certain death. Good to know one's options."

You have probably observed, good Reader, that escapes in movies are always exciting and dashing and sometimes *jolly.* They have thrilling titles like *The Perilous Breakout at Bleakstone Prison* or *The Fantastic Flight of the So-and-So Gang.* There are often a couple of terrific explosions, and usually a dramatic gunfight, and sometimes a bit of slipping on banana peels to provide comic relief.

Anastasia had not, in her entire stay at St. Agony's, seen a single banana.

This worried her.

"First things first!" Ollie declared. "Let's form our secret getaway crew. And then we can call our adventure

The Daring Escape of Whoever We Are." Apparently he had watched a number of action films, too.

To Anastasia, founder and sole representative of the Francie Dewdrop Admiration Society, belonging to a club with more than one member seemed pretty good. And belonging to a *secret* club—with top-secret *Shadowboys*—seemed even better. "All right," she said. "What's it called?"

"I don't know yet," Ollie admitted.

Quentin strummed a silvery melody on the bars of his cage. "How about the Bog Street Trio?"

"That's not right at all," Ollie said. "It sounds like one of your musical groups. There needs to be a sense of danger and excitement! And our name should be a little scary, too. Strike dread in the hearts of kidnappers, and all that. *I know!* The Ghastly Gingerbread League!"

"What does gingerbread have to do with anything?" Quentin demanded.

"Run, run, as fast as you can! You can't catch me—I'm the gingerbread man!" Ollie sang. "I always liked that story. And it fits our situation! The gingerbread man is running away from a nasty old lady!"

"But don't you know how it ends?" Quentin asked. "The gingerbread boy gets crunched by a fox!"

"What?" Ollie's eyes rounded. "But—"

"You always ran off in the middle of the book to go bake," Quentin reminded him.

"Well, I got inspired," Ollie said. "I'm going to be a top-rate pastry chef when I grow up," he informed Anastasia. "Tell her about my gingerbread houses, Q."

"Ollie's gingerbread houses *are* scrumptious," Quentin allowed.

"And *huge*. I even made a gingerbread St. Basil's Cathedral," Ollie went on.

"Have you seen the kitchen here?" Anastasia asked. "It has all kinds of fancy cooking stuff. They even have a jelly mold shaped like the asylum."

Ollie perked up. "Really? Let's go there now! I can make us a Bundt!"

"We're plotting our great escape," Anastasia pointed out. "And we haven't even come up with a name for our posse."

"The Ghastly Gingerbread League seems pretty good to me," Ollie grumbled.

"I do like *league*," Anastasia said. "That sounds impressive."

"And capable," Quentin said. "A league would be quite capable of launching a Daring Escape from two horrible kidnappers."

"No more *Dreadful beastly boys should be seen and not heard*," Ollie mimicked Prim.

"No more *Dig that hole faster, you beastly teenager!*" Quentin said.

"We'll show Prim and Prude just how beastly we can be!" Ollie grinned and clacked his poisonous teeth.

"That's it!" Anastasia cried. *"The League of Beastly Dreadfuls!"*

"The League of Beastly Dreadfuls." Quentin nodded. "It has a certain ring to it."

Ollie cheered. "I like it, too! *The League of Beastly Dreadfuls!"*

Anastasia thought of the spidery script on Lucy Pinkerton's photo. *TO THE DREADFUL.* Well, she was going *to the Dreadful,* all right, but not whatever *Dreadful* Prim and Prude had plotted for her. Hopefully. "Let's pinkie-swear on it."

They clinched pinkies.

"And now," Ollie said, "we have to plan that Daring Escape."

"We must leave in three nights exactly," Quentin said.

"Why do we have to leave at *night*?" Anastasia asked, imagining the Creature smacking its lips in the starless Dread Woods.

"It's dark at night," Quentin answered. "Easier to slip away unnoticed. Only one kidnapper will be watching from the glass tower. They take shifts so they can sleep."

"Oh," Anastasia said. "But why *three* nights?"

"Because that's the night of the full moon, and that's when we Shadowfolk are at our best," Quentin said.

"I don't want to wait three nights!" Ollie complained. "Full moon or not, can't we just run away?"

"It isn't that simple, Pudding," Quentin said. "Prim and Prude lock Anastasia up every night and mirror me into my room. And didn't you notice the electric fence when they brought you here? Very tall, and tipped with mirrors. Besides, I won't be able to umbrate with this thing on." He rattled the head cage. "That's why the kidnappers stuck it on me."

Anastasia pondered the iron padlock dangling from the metal collar. "Maybe we can pick that. Let's see if there's anything useful in the Treatment Room."

Unfortunately, not a single pick or needle or other pointy instrument in the Treatment Room could twitch open the padlock. Anastasia scowled and flung down an authentic Victorian lobotomy drill, mentally crossing "expert lock picker" from her detective-veterinarian-artist résumé.

"Let's saw it off," Quentin urged.

"But if Prim and Prude see that your head cage is mangled, they'll just put a new one on you," Anastasia reasoned. "We need to get it off without them noticing."

Ollie let out a howl and hiccup from where he knelt by the toy cupboard. His back was to them, but his shoulders jiggled with little *boohoohoo*s.

"It's all right, Ollie," Anastasia reassured him. "We'll figure something out."

"What?" Ollie sniffled. "No, I just finished the first fairy tale in this book. And the princess winds up locked in a tower! That's not how the story ends in my book at home." He swiveled his face back toward them. His eyes were wet and his cheeks gleamed with mercurial streaks. The silvery stuff dripped down to his sweater and sizzled the woolly loops. *Hsssst!*

"Ollie!" Anastasia shrilled. "What's on your face? It's burning your sweater! Did you get into those bottles of Victorian medicine?"

"They're just tears," Ollie said. "Oh, the poor princess, locked up like that."

"Shadowtears burn," Quentin explained. "Through fabrics and most metals—but not silver, of course. You should see Ollie's pillowcase at home. It looks like moths got into it. He's always crying when he reads bedtime stories."

"Shut up, Quentin," Ollie said, wiping his face with the back of his sleeve. *Hsssst!* The woolly weft began to unravel.

Anastasia's gaze leapfrogged from Ollie's frayed sweater to the padlock swaying from Quentin's cage.

"Ollie," she said. "Let's see that book."

"And then," Anastasia read in her most sinister story-time voice, "the little mermaid bade her prince farewell and leapt into the sea."

"No!" Ollie cried. "That isn't how it's supposed to end! The little mermaid marries the prince and they live happily ever after!"

"But she didn't," Anastasia said mournfully. "Not in the real story. Nope. No happily ever after there."

Hsssst! Hsssst!

"Quick!" Anastasia said. "Use this!" She uncorked Miss Viola's tear catcher. "Hold it to the corner of your eye."

"It's all so sad!" Ollie howled. "The poor mermaid. She died for *LUUUUURVE*."

"Ollie?" Anastasia whispered. "Do you think you could wail a little more quietly? We don't want Prim and Prude to hear us."

"Couldn't you make me cry tears of joy instead?" Ollie grumped. "They're just as sizzly."

"Really?" Anastasia said. "You should have mentioned that. Maybe we can make you laugh until you cry."

"I know a limerick," Quentin said. "Listen closely, Ollie:

A bachelor from Timbuktu
Met an amorous ape at the zoo.
To Las Vegas they fled;
In a chapel they wed,
And now spend their days flinging poo."

Ollie giggled.

"Not funny enough," Anastasia said. "Try another one, Quentin."

He cleared his throat.

"An old perfumer from the Bronx
Grew increasingly obsessed with skunks.
'Check beneath the tail
For a singular smell!
I could sit and inhale it for months!'"

"It's a nice rhyme," Ollie said, "but it isn't really *hilarious*."

The Treatment Room was quiet for a minute.

"Tickle Monster!" Quentin cried, pouncing on Ollie and grabbling his ribs. Ollie squealed in delight. *Hsssst! Hsssst!*

"You're wasting tears!" Anastasia said. "Quick, catch them!"

Ollie sprawled on the tiled floor, panting. Quentin held up the tear catcher with satisfaction. "That should do the trick."

Anastasia plucked the vial from him. She tilted it above the padlock. *Hsssst!*

"It's working!" she cried. "It's burning through the shackle!"

"Hooray!" Ollie whooped.

Anastasia popped the padlock and swung the collar back. "Freedom!" she proclaimed, pulling the cage off Quentin's head.

"Oh, thank goodness!" He clawed his blotchy neck.

"You'll have to wear the cage in front of Prim and Prude," Anastasia reminded him. "We can't let them realize that you can take it off. Ugh, you have a terrible rash!"

"It's the silver," Ollie said. "It makes us break out in awful welts."

Anastasia jolted. She yanked Granny McCrumpet's necklace out of her shirt. "The kidnappers gave me this silver chain," she said. "And they keep checking me for a rash."

"Take that necklace off right now!" Ollie said.

"But I'm not itchy." Anastasia slumped on the floor and stared at the ruby winking on the silver heart. Why had Prim and Prude kidnapped *her*? She wasn't a Shadowchild. She was absolutely ordinary in every way. What about the other children whose glum faces glowered from the walls of Room Thirteen? Had any of those kids been magical? Why did the Watchers snatch *magical* children to feed to the Creature? Or did they just stumble upon Ollie by accident, and decided to use him for his Shadowsilk? Perhaps that's why Prim and Prude had fed him so many cakes— they were trying to plump him up, so his silken suit would be bigger!

And Ollie was the perfect victim for nefarious

Hansel-and-Gretel-type schemes. He was clutching his tummy at that very moment.

"I'm so hungry," he lamented. "Do you have any candy?"

As you may or may not remember, the day of Anastasia's first premonition of doom happened to be the day after Halloween, and her satchel was still jumbled with crumpled wrappers torn from lollipops and chocolate Scrummy bars. The only sugarplum that had escaped her sweet tooth was the sour watermelon taffy, a flavor she couldn't bear for reasons to be discussed later in our story. She now offered these sour watermelon globs to her fellow Beastly Dreadfuls, and they continued to hatch their scheme.

"We still need to figure out your door," Ollie mumbled, his cheeks puffed like a chipmunk's.

"Prude stashes all the keys in her purse," Quentin mused. "But she always keeps it with her."

"And even if we somehow managed to steal the key," Anastasia said, "she'd figure it out as soon as they went to lock me in my moldy room again."

"Mold," Ollie garbled. "Mold!" He sputtered the taffy out onto his palm and peered at the green lump. He poked it with his finger. He smiled at them. "I have solved the problem of the door key," he announced. "Quentin, don't swallow that taffy! We're going to need it."

And then he told them his idea.

"Ollie, that's ingenious!" Quentin declared. "Now we

just have to concoct a way to get Prude's purse for a few minutes."

"It's hard thinking on an empty stomach," Ollie bellyached. "Anastasia, don't you have *any* other sweets? Did you see any chocolate in the kitchen?"

"Not in the kitchen," Anastasia replied. "But there's a Miracle Choco-Laxative bar in Room Nine if you're interested."

"Choco-laxatives?" Quentin echoed, his Adam's apple doing a little double Dutch. "*That's it!* I know how to distract the kidnappers!"

❦ 20 ❦

The Triumphant Zonk

UP IN ANASTASIA'S room, the League of Beastly Dreadfuls tore the wrappers from the sour watermelon taffies, one by one. Within a few minutes they had shucked exactly forty-two taffies, and they lined them up in a revolting green row.

Next Anastasia unpeeled the paper jacket from Dr. Whistlewind's Miracle Choco-Laxative (swiped from Room Nine). It looked just like any normal candy bar, with the exception of the word *Whistlewind* stamped in teensy letters on each chocolate brick. Anastasia licked her forefinger and smudged the cursive impressions off every rectangle.

"Brilliant," Quentin said.

"Thank you." Anastasia selected the least ragged of the pink Scrummy wrappers and folded it around the Miracle

Choco-Laxative. It didn't fit perfectly, but it looked pretty good. She slipped the laxative bar into her pocket.

She checked her watch. "It's getting close to lunchtime."

"Ready!" Ollie grabbed a taffy. "Set!"

The next task was particularly odious to Anastasia, but it was necessary.

"Go!" Quentin commanded.

Anastasia pinched her nostrils shut and put the taffy into her mouth. She chewed. Oh, how she chewed! She chewed until the taffy was very soft, and then she spit it out and put it back on the floor. The Beastly Dreadfuls chewed each and every taffy, sticking them together to create one big gob.

"Well done," Ollie said.

"Ugh." Anastasia wiped a smear of green drool from her chin and squashed the taffy into her satchel.

"We'll meet you downstairs," Quentin whispered. Anastasia nodded and slipped out the door.

You can probably guess what our brave hero planned to do with the chocolate laxative bar. She was going to zonk her "aunties." Now, deliberately feeding laxatives to some poor, unsuspecting soul is bad form. It's morally unsavory. But Prim and Prude were diabolical child-snatchers, and the usual rules of What Is Nice and What Is Not Nice didn't apply to them.

Anastasia trotted into the dining room and sat down at her normal place. The kidnappers were already sloshing Mystery Lumps around with their spoons.

"I'm telling you, I saw a whistle-bottomed whoopsie-will!" Prude said.

"Nonsense! It was a blue-pimpled nincompoop," Prim retorted.

Anastasia withdrew from her pocket the laxative bar crinkling in the Scrummy paper. She smiled and tore the wrapper and broke off one of the chocolate squares.

"Well, a blue-pimpled— What's that?" Prude asked, her hedgehoggy eyes latching on to the chocolate.

"I just found this candy bar," Anastasia said. "It's from Halloween. It's been down at the bottom of my satchel all this time!"

"Candy bar?" Prim said.

"It's a Scrummy," Anastasia said, flashing the wrapper at them. "My very favorite. I could eat Scrummies all day. Isn't it wonderful that I found this one?"

"Give that to me this instant!" Prim cried.

"Oh, but, Auntie—"

"Chocolate will rot your teeth," Prim said. "Hand it over, dearie." She wiggled her fingers, the silver eyeball twinkling on her pinkie.

Anastasia sighed and pressed the laxative into the old woman's palm.

"Of course," Prim said, champing her metal jaws, "chocolate won't rot *our* teeth, will it, Prudie?"

Anastasia's young soul throbbed with hope. *Please,* she

thought. *Please please please let this work.* The laxative was, after all, probably one hundred years old. Perhaps the child-snatchers would throw the chocolate down in disgust after one bite.

"Shall we?" giggled Prude.

"Please don't!" Anastasia protested in a great show of distress. "It's *my* Halloween candy, after all. Please don't eat my Scrummy bar."

This is called reverse psychology, which is the art of convincing your adversary to do something by urging them *not* to do it. Certain stubborn and contrary people are very susceptible to reverse psychology. Anastasia, of course, really *wanted* Prim and Prude to devour every last morsel of the laxative. But she couldn't tell them that. If she had presented the odious child-snatchers with the candy bar and begged them to eat it, Prim and Prude would most likely have refused to do so, simply in the spirit of being difficult.

"Little orphans don't get to tell adults what to do," Prim said briskly. She snapped the bar in two and gave half to Prude, and then they both gobbled the chocolate down.

"Delicious," declared Prude.

"Scrumptious," agreed Prim. "Now, Anastasia, eat your Mystery Lumps."

Anastasia poked her Lumps with her spoon and silently counted: *one* mashed potato, *two* mashed potato, *three* mashed potato . . .

Prim's teacup clattered to its saucer. Anastasia's gaze snapped from her uneaten Lumps to the ancient biddy's face, which had gone white as a sheet.

"Why, Primrose!" exclaimed Prude. "Whatever is the matter?"

"I . . . oh, dear . . . ," Prim mumbled, clutching the edge of the table. A dreadful noise rumbled from the seat of her chair. It sounded like a tuba being readied for the symphony.

"Primrose!" cried Prude. "At the table! Disgusting!"

"Oh, shut up!" Prim wailed as another stonking great noise rumbled forth. "Can't you see I'm ill?"

"My goodness!" said Prude.

Vrooooom! growled Prim's chair.

"Shocking!" Prude exclaimed. "Never in my life— Oh, my." Her eyes widened as a colossal raspberry erupted from beneath her fur coat.

Blaaaat!

Tooooooooooot!

Primrose howled a word that is not fit to be printed within the pages of the respectable volume you now hold, and she leapt from her chair and dashed hollering out of the room. Prudence followed suit, clutching her bottom.

If Anastasia had merely zonked her kidnappers as a prank, she would have been hugging herself to keep her sides from splitting with delirious laughter. However, the laxatives were an imperative step in the Beastly Dreadfuls' path to escape, and she had serious business ahead of her. She didn't have time to sit around chuckling. She nicked around the table and seized Prude's purse, abandoned in all the excitement. Unclasping the silver jaws, she peered inside.

There was the usual old lady paraphernalia, like crumpled tissues and ancient lip salves. There was the screwdriver the kidnappers used to unmirror the entry to Quentin's room. There were peppermints, of course. There was also a book featuring upon its cover a rugged, mustachioed man clutching a wrinkled damsel to his chest.

"*The Handsome Rogue Who Fell in Love with the Older Lady*," Anastasia whispered. "*A Sizzling and Plausible Tale of May–December Romance.*"

Quentin and Ollie burst into the dining room. "Did you find it?"

"Look at this!" Anastasia said, brandishing a small box labeled DR. PALSY'S MONOBROW WAXING KIT. "Prude must have a monobrow!"

"Ick!" Ollie said.

"And I bet Prim has one, too!" Anastasia said.

"Hurry!" Quentin urged.

Anastasia rummaged through the hodgepodge until her fingers closed around the manacle dangling with all the keys to all the doors in St. Agony's Asylum. She squinted at the little silver numbers until she saw eleven, and she slid it off the hoop. "Here, Ollie."

"Give me that jailer's ring," Quentin said. "I'll go unlock the kitchen door." He dashed from the dining room.

Anastasia pulled the taffy clod from her satchel. It was still warm and pliable from the Beastly Dreadfuls' expert chewing. Ollie squished the key down into the green lump. Then, using the tippity-end of his fingernail, he ever-so-carefully prized the key out of the sour watermelon stamp.

Joy! Huzzah! Anastasia marveled at the beautiful imprint left behind by the key, her heart leaping and cart-wheeling.

"Victory for the League of Beastly Dreadfuls!" Ollie crowed.

"Shake a leg," Quentin panted, scrambling back into the dining room. "We have to move to phase two before the kidnappers return." He flung Prude's key ring to Anastasia. She threaded number eleven back onto the metal hoop and shoved the clanking jumble deep into Prude's purse.

The League sprinted down the hallway to a large door. Quentin flung it open. "I'll keep watch out here. Be as fast as you can."

Ollie pulled a stool up to the stove and took a metal pot down from the wall and clunked it onto one of the burners. There was still some water sloshing in the kidnappers' tea-kettle. He poured this water into the pot. When bubbles began to froth and fizz, he said, "The sugar, please."

Anastasia fetched the sugar bowl and handed it to Ollie.

He plucked out glittering cubes, one by one, and plopped them into the burbling water.

Watching her fellow Dreadful simmer the sugar, Anastasia strained her eardrums for a jangle from Quentin's cage. If one of the child-snatchers caught them in the kitchen, their intricate escape plan would be dashed to bits.

"How's the paste coming?" she asked.

"Gloopier by the moment," Ollie reported. "Do you think I'd have time to bake a cake before we go?"

"No time for cakes!"

Ollie gazed at the scraggly trees outside. "It's December," he sighed. "Perhaps I could make a gingerbread lunatic asylum this year. I could use marshmallow fluff for the padded rooms down in the basement."

"Hurry, Ollie," Anastasia said.

"You can't hurry confectioners," Ollie said. But he held up the spoon and eyed the white paste. His face lit up with a smile. "It's ready now."

Anastasia took the taffy mold out of her satchel and laid it flat on the wooden counter. Arms trembling, Ollie hefted the pot and tilted it above the taffy. Anastasia watched anxiously as the sizzling hot sugar goop oozed down to fill the dent the key had left behind. She was afraid that the boiling sugar might melt the mold, but it did not. It filled the impression and bubbled in the shape of a Victorian key.

Ollie picked up the taffy mold with the delicacy of a jeweler handling a Fabergé egg. Lightly, with the pad of his index finger, he prodded the sugar paste.

"Do you really think this will work?" Anastasia asked.

Ollie nodded, handing her the taffy. "Hard as a jawbreaker."

Anastasia pocketed the mold. "But I thought jawbreakers had cement in them."

Ollie shot her a scornful look.

"Some kind of delicious, edible cement," Anastasia added hastily.

Shockingly, Reader, jawbreakers do not contain cement. They are made of sugar mixed with water, cooked together at a very high temperature. That's it.

"Now lock the door behind me and ride the dumbwaiter down to the basement," Anastasia told Ollie. They clasped pinkies, and she sidled into the hallway.

"Just in time," Quentin said. "I heard footsteps on the stairs!"

Anastasia skedaddled back to the dining room and leapt into her chair. She picked up her spoon. No one would have guessed that she had just committed a daring and defiant act with her Beastly comrades.

"Anastasia!" Prim lurched through the entryway. "Get to Room Eleven, dear. Prude and I are having—a lady never mentions—powdering our—anyway, we can't watch you, so you're going to have to play in your room today."

"Poor aunties," Anastasia said.

Thus we learn that, like elephants, laxative bars are best eaten one bite at a time—and never, never, *never* gobbled down all at once.

21

Squeak 'n' Poo

ANASTASIA REMOVED THE mold from her pocket and set it on the floor, and then she used her bent safety pin to ease the sugar key out of its little key-shaped hollow, worried the entire time that it might crumble into tiny crystals. It did not. The key was lustrous and lovely. It sparkled like snow in the candlelight.

Holding her breath, Anastasia inserted the sugar key into the keyhole. Would it break? She twisted it ever so slowly. She rattled it. However, the lock wouldn't budge.

"Biscuit crumbs!" Removing the key, she peered down at it. Bits of sugar clumped against one of the teeth. Anastasia chipped at them with her fingernail, but the key was too hard. It *was* strong as cement. She felt certain that the botched tooth was keeping the key from doing its important work. If only she had a file to shape the key!

And then she realized she had something even better than a file.

She had her tongue.

She carefully licked at the key, just as you would lick a jawbreaker in the safety of your own home. Delicious! Anastasia shaped the key one scrumptious lick at a time, until it was perfectly smooth. She fit it in the keyhole.

Click.

Anastasia turned the knob. The door opened just an inch before tugging against the chain. She pulled the door shut again and turned the key. She jiggled the knob. It stuck fast. She unlocked it again, certain that the sound of the key shifting the tumblers was the most beautiful sound in the entire world.

There remained the chain, but she had a plan for that. She scampered to her satchel and took out the powerful magnet shaped like a U, pilfered from the Treatment Room. She held it against the door and slowly ran it up and down. It latched to the wood, leech-like, a couple of feet above the knob. Anastasia wiggled the ends of the U. She could hear tiny clinks on the other side of the wood as the chain's bulbous end clanked through the little metal track attaching it to the door.

Clunk.

She pushed the door open. The chain dangled harmlessly from its bolt on the wall.

Anastasia grinned.

She had just swallowed her first bite of elephant.

Glaring at her bowl of Mystery Lumps at breakfast the following morning, Anastasia stewed that if Prim and Prude were fattening Ollie up for his Shadowsilk, it was only fair that they treat *her* to something good before trying to feed her to the Creature in the Woods.

Prude was also squinting into her bowl. "Prim," she said, "are we eating our Mystery Lumps with chocolate sprinkles now?"

"Of course not," Prim replied. "Chocolate sprinkles are an extravagance this household cannot afford."

Prude scooted her spectacles to the end of her nose and scrutinized her spoon. "Why, those aren't sprinkles at all," she said slowly. "They're—"

"Look!" Anastasia cried. "By the pickle jar!"

They gaped in speechless surprise at the trim little figure standing at attention in the middle of the breakfast table. He gazed straight at Anastasia, eyes twinkling and alert, and then scampered bold as brass right up to Prude's teacup and put his small pink hands on the rim and stuck his whiskery nose down into the milk-clouded tea. Prude stared at him

in pale revulsion, then looked back at the little brown specks in her spoon.

"Mouse droppings!" she screamed.

"Filthy, plague-spreading vermin!" Prim screeched. "Kill it! Kill it!"

"No!" Anastasia hollered, but the umbrella was already crashing down on the tabletop, smashing the teacup into smithereens. The umbrella did not, however, smash the mouse. The mouse was a splendid acrobat. He leapt away unscathed. Prim squawked as the umbrella sprang open, then struggled to force it back closed.

"Vermin!" Prude shrieked, snatching up a fork and stabbing it down again and again as the mouse cartwheeled between the dishes. "Hold still and let me kill you!"

"Stop it!" Anastasia yelled, jumping out of her seat. "Stop!"

"He's getting away!" Prim shrilled.

Crash! Smash! The umbrella whacked down, demolishing bowls and teacups and sending poop-sprinkled globs of Mystery Lumps spattering into everyone's faces. The nimble mouse eluded every attack. He was a fine mouse indeed, and Anastasia brimmed with admiration for him. She went limp with relief when the mouse finally leapt from the table to the floor and zipped out of the room.

"Disgusting!" Prim seethed.

"Despicable!" hissed Prude.

"It was only a little mouse," Anastasia protested.

"*Only a little mouse!*" Prim blazed. "Look at this table! It's a complete wreck! All our lovely dishes smashed!"

"Well," Anastasia pointed out, "*you* did that, after all."

"That rotten scrounger used our breakfast for a chamber pot!" Prude wailed. "Just the thought of that nasty brute trespassing through our kitchen makes my skin itch! *Oooooh,* do I have the creepy crawlies!"

No sooner had she plunged her hand down her collar to scratch, however, than she yanked it back out and began wrestling from her coat as though it were on fire. "*Oooooh!*" she gasped. "*Ooooooh!*" The coat fell to the floor and Prude hopped away from it and up onto her chair with surprising agility for such a frail old person.

"By gosh," Prim exclaimed, pointing at the coat with the umbrella, "it's moving!"

The coat bristled and rustled and fluttered.

"It's alive!" Prude caterwauled, her face turning white. "It's come back to life! I *felt* it! Kill it!"

"Don't be daft," Prim snapped, but her face was white, too.

Little tufts of fur began to quiver right off the coat and

scamper and jump and squeak and zoom over the marble floor like fuzzy toy cars.

"Mice!" Prim whacked the floor. "Mice! We're under siege!"

And she began clomping and kicking and saying a lot of impolite words. Her evil jitterbugging and foul language did not bother the mice at all. They were clever and capable. They scaled Prim's skinny ankles and shins and scurried all the way up her skirt. When they tired of that, they swarmed out of her collar and somersaulted down to the breakfast table, prancing among the shards of china and spatters of Mystery Lumps.

And then, quick as a wink, the mice were gone. Nobody even saw where they went. All that remained of the great mouse invasion were thousands of tiny brown mouse missiles.

Screaming did not help.

Stomping did not work. Nor did threats.

Nor, for that matter, did mousetraps. The clever mice turned up their whiskered noses at the bits of peppermint clamped in the traps' metal jaws. They burrowed into the sugar bowl and munched the antique furniture and gnawed through the kidnappers' knitting. They even got into the harpsichord. Anastasia lifted the sheet and watched the keys fidget up and down as though a ghost were pressing them.

Of course, it was really just the mice jumping on the hammers and wires in the harpsichord's belly. It made a wonderful ruckus.

The mice also made a good distraction. Prim and Prude were so busy flinging teacups and walloping their umbrella that Anastasia had plenty of time to slip down to Dr. Grungewhiff's office to scheme with her fellow Beastly Dreadfuls.

"Look at this!" Ollie said, twirling a silk stocking like a slingshot. It was another scrap of Shadowsilk, this time sloughed off his leg.

Anastasia grabbed the toe. "Tug-of-war!"

She yanked her end of the stocking, marveling as the silk stretched out of the office and all the way down the corridor. The shadow sock pulled taut, but it didn't snap. "Amazing!" Anastasia skipped back into the mirrored room.

"Stop playing," Quentin scolded. "We have to conspire."

"I love conspiring," Ollie said.

"Good, because our Daring Escape is tomorrow night," Quentin said.

Anastasia and Ollie gulped.

"Now that you have the sugar key, Anastasia, you can let yourself out of Room Eleven and come unmirror me from Room Thirty-Eight," Quentin went on. "Ollie, we'll drag one of these mirrors ajar for you, so you can come up the dumbwaiter and meet us."

"Freedom!" Ollie huzzahed. "Oh, I can't wait to get out of this awful basement!"

"But we still have to get out of the asylum," Quentin reminded him. "There's a combination lock on the front door."

"Anastasia, you're not a safecracker, are you?" Ollie asked.

"Nope. Sorry."

"We have to come up with another escape route," Quentin said.

"What about breaking a window?" Ollie suggested.

"Too noisy," said Quentin.

"Well, poop." Ollie slumped and began humming "Ballad of the Lovelorn Beluga." Anastasia closed her eyes and listened to the melody, remembering the days when she had wondered whether Quentin's peculiar saw music was the sound of wind piping through the chimneys.

Her eyelids snapped open. "I know how to get out!"

And she told the Shadowboys her idea.

"That sounds a bit dangerous," Ollie said.

"A *bit*!" Quentin cried. "Anastasia could break her neck!"

"It's the only way," Anastasia said. "Remember: escape or die trying."

Quentin drummed his fingers on his knee. "All right," he gave in. "But we still have the problem of Prim and Prude."

"We have to get them away from the windows to give us time to get to the fence. But," Anastasia mused, "we're out of chocolate laxative."

"We only need to distract Prude," Quentin said. "She'll be the one on guard tomorrow night."

"How do you know that?" Anastasia asked.

"I eavesdrop a lot," Quentin said. "I'm pretty brilliant at it."

The room was silent as they pondered distractions.

"We'll have to improvise," Ollie finally concluded. "Just like when I used nighty-night cough syrup instead of vanilla in my coffee cake."

"Ollie!" Quentin scolded. "You must promise *never* to put medicine in your baking! It's *dangerous!*"

"It was *coffee* cake," Ollie argued. "It seemed sensible to me. Besides, all great pastry chefs experiment with new and unusual ingredients."

"Not medicine!"

"Maybe you're right," Ollie admitted. "Everyone was falling asleep at the table."

Anastasia perked up. *"Medicine!"* she cried. *"Dr. Bluster's Patented Sleep Preparation of Most Sleepful Sleep!"*

"Dr. Whozit's whatsit?" Ollie asked.

"Just one drop would knock a rhinoceros on its rump," Anastasia said. "That's what the label says. Prim and Prude use it on their peppermints. And I'm sure that's what they put into your tea, Quentin. There's a whole bottle of it in their secret parlor."

"The fiends!" Quentin swore.

"Quite right," Ollie agreed. "Very fiendish, those two. We should pinch that bottle and pour it right down the drain!"

"No, Ollie," Anastasia said firmly. "We should pinch that bottle and pour it right into Prim and Prude's tea."

"Good thinking!" Ollie cheered. "Now we don't need any distraction at all! We can just clobber those child-snatchers with sleeping stuff and stroll out the door without so much as a how-do-you-do."

Quentin scratched his spotty neck. "What about the poodles? And the fence?"

"And the Creature?" Anastasia added.

"We'll umbrate," Ollie said, "and if the poodles try to get close to Anastasia, we'll bite them. Same with the Creature."

"That doesn't solve the problem of the fence," Quentin said.

Anastasia checked her watch. "I'd better get back upstairs," she said. "It's getting late, and Prim and Prude will be looking for me."

They trapped Ollie in the circle of mirrors, just in case the Watchers trotted downstairs to bring him another cupcake of diabolical intent. At the dumbwaiter, Quentin and Anastasia clasped pinkies. Then she hauled herself up to the second floor.

"Anastasia!"

"Oh!" Anastasia gulped as she stepped out of Room Nine. Prim and Prude were standing in the gloomy hallway.

"What were you doing in there, moppet?" Prim asked. "We told you not to go into rooms with closed doors."

"I—I was looking for a—a ladder so I could really get at those cobwebs hanging from the chandeliers," Anastasia stuttered.

"Oh," said Prude. "Well, that can wait until tomorrow. It's getting close to dark, and as you know, Nice Little Girls—"

"Are in bed before dark," Anastasia interjected. "Yes, I know. I was—I'm sleepy, anyway."

"I'm sure you're not too sleepy to smile for just one little picture," Prim said, pulling a big old clunker of a camera from behind her back.

"We realized today that we don't have a single photograph of our darling great-niece!" Prude piped up.

"But—" Anastasia squirmed as she thought of the photographs wincing from the walls of Room Thirteen. "There isn't enough light in here—and I haven't brushed my hair this week—"

"Nonsense," twittered Prude, her fingers darting forward to fiddle with the silver chain at Anastasia's collar. "You look darling."

"Besides," Prim added, "this camera has a heck of a flash. You'll feel like someone threw a Molotov cocktail right up your nose."

Prude beamed. "Now stand up straight and say *cheese*."

"Cheese," Anastasia croaked.

Pop! Artificial light dazzled the hallway. Anastasia was still blinking away the sparkles on her eyeballs when Prim and Prude hustled her into Room Eleven and clunked the locks into place.

Fear flooded her freckled body. She knew just how she would look in that picture—ill at ease, as though she were wearing wet socks or underpants that didn't quite fit, or had just had a tooth pulled.

In other words: just like the other children in the photographs in the secret parlor.

She shivered, glad the Beastly Dreadfuls would be launching their Daring Escape the next night.

Now, she thought, it was time to move to the next step in their brilliant plan. She removed the magnet and sugar key from her satchel and put them to work. She stole into the hallway and hurried down and around and up and through the maze of corridors to Room Thirteen. Looking over her shoulder to make sure the hallway was empty, she peeled back the wallpaper to reveal the keyhole and let herself in.

The sad little faces of the Watchers' young victims gazed at her as she tiptoed to pilfer Dr. Bluster's Patented Sleep Preparation. She pilfered the paintbrush, too.

"Goodbye," she whispered to the photographs. "I won't see you again."

Dozens upon dozens of sad eyes watched as she slipped from the room.

❧ 22 ❧

The Mouse Destroyer

"**WELL, AUNTIE PRIM,**" Anastasia said, "your dream has finally come true."

Prim lowered her binoculars, her mouth pulled into an angry line. "What on earth are you talking about?"

Anastasia grinned. "St. Agony's is a bed-and-breakfast, just like you wanted." Feeling less inclined to good manners on this, the day of the Beastly Dreadfuls' Daring Escape, she continued, "A bed-and-breakfast for mice. We could call it . . . the Squeak 'n' Poo."

"Stop smiling," Prim snapped. "This is a serious matter."

"We must call an exterminator," said Prude. "There's no way around it."

"We can't afford an exterminator," Prim retorted. "Besides . . ."

The old ladies' eyes drifted toward the glass walls. The Dread Woods were just a dark blur beyond the fog curling against the glass, but Anastasia knew what they were thinking about. The Creature.

Anastasia gazed into the gardens, too. Down among the topiaries, Quentin was busy shoveling. He couldn't let the kidnappers know that Anastasia had no intention of winding up in the bone garden. The shovel lashed into the air, flinging mud right onto the nose of a shaggy giraffe (or brachiosaur). As Anastasia watched, the hole deepened until only the bell on Quentin's head cage was visible.

"I'm sure the mice will get tired of bothering us and just go away," Prim said, lifting her binoculars back to her face.

"I'm sure you're right, Auntie," Anastasia said, smothering a giggle. The mice weren't going to just go away. They waltzed around St. Agony's Asylum like they owned the place. There was even, at that very moment, a mouse sitting on top of Prude's head, surveying the glass tower with lordly curiosity. Prude held her chipped teacup with trembling hands but did not drink from it. There was no sugar, because the mice had devoured it all.

Anastasia admired the mice from the bottom of her soul. They almost distracted her from the nerves jangling her tummy. Within a few hours, the League of Beastly Dreadfuls would launch their getaway. She had already sneaked down to Dr. Grungewhiff's office after lunch to free Ollie

from his looking-glass clinker. She had tucked his music box into her satchel, since he wouldn't be able to carry it once he umbrated. They hugged, trying not to let their fear show.

For, tenderhearted Reader, Anastasia *was* fearful. She tallied the flaws in their escape plan. Poodles. Fence. And once past the fence, the umbrated Shadowboys could elude whatever heart-munching Creature lurked in the Dread Woods, but Anastasia would have to plod through the wintry December night as her absolutely ordinary self. The Dreadfuls planned to run until they stumbled upon the nearest town, but how far away might that be? If worse came to worst, the boys could whiz home to faraway Melancholy Falls and get help—but that would mean leaving Anastasia behind in the forest. Alone. With the Creature.

"I can't live like this any longer!" Prude wailed. "I can't eat, because the filthy vermin have befouled all the food. I can't sleep, because as soon as I lie down in bed, the mice jump up and down on my bosom like it's a trampoline."

"Now, Prudie," Prim said, "you know I would like nothing better than to get rid of these rodents. However, like chocolate sprinkles and funerals, the services of a pest exterminator simply cost too much. And besides—"

But whatever wise thing Prim was about to say next was interrupted by three loud knocks. Everyone jumped a bit, even the mouse, who scurried down Prude's wooly cardigan and vamoosed into the gloom.

Prude set her teacup down. "Was that . . ."

"Someone at the front door," Prim said.

Prim and Prude stared at each other with something like shock. They were, Anastasia realized, *afraid,* and a shiver ran down her spine. Or was it a mouse? It was difficult to tell these days.

"I didn't see anybody out there," Prude said.

"It's very cloudy today," Prim said grimly. "Bad visibility."

Three more knocks.

Prim pulled the brim of her hat down and set the binoculars on a crooked little end table scattered with mouse droppings. "Well," she said, "we'll just have to see who it is."

"Maybe it's someone selling vacuums," Anastasia suggested.

They descended the spiral staircase and twisted through the moldy corridors to the entrance hall. "Anastasia, go to your room," Prim said. "And close the door."

Anastasia scuttled up the green-carpeted staircase, passing the monobrowed portraits and thumping up to the landing. She did not, however, go down the long hall. She pressed tight against the wall, crouching in a shadow. Who, she wondered, could be at the front door? Perhaps it was Mr. and Mrs. Drybread! Perhaps they were here to rescue Ollie and Quentin!

Or maybe it was even Fred McCrumpet!

On the other hand . . . maybe the Creature was standing

at the front door that very minute, its frightful bottom reflected in the mirror bolted to the front porch. Was it too hungry for Anastasia's heart to wait politely in the woods?

She shrank into her coat, feeling a mouse wiggle against her side.

Prim and Prude exchanged a grim look. Prim held up her long knitting needle and nodded. Prude twisted the combination lock and cracked the door open.

"Who are you?" Prim demanded. "And how did you get through the gates?"

Anastasia sagged in relief. Whoever it was, it must not have been the Creature.

"The gates?" came a manly voice. "Why, they were open. I do hope I'm not trespassing."

"You are," Prim said. "We have those gates to keep strange men from bothering us. Now please go away."

"Good day," fluttered Prude, but the visitor stuck his foot between the door and jamb before the biddy could shut him out. Anastasia saw four large fingertips peep around the edge of the door, and then it swung back into the Great Hall.

The intruder was so tall that he almost filled the doorway. He had a thick manly neck, and a manly cleft in the center of his manly chin. His glorious ginger-colored mustache curled back from his upper lip like a triumphant banner. He wore a military uniform twinkling with brass buttons and buckles and star-shaped studs, and he was carrying a large suitcase.

"Greetings!" he said. "Allow me to introduce myself. I am the Baron von Bilgeworth, Mouse Destroyer Extraordinaire."

"Mouse Destroyer!" the sisters gasped.

"Yes indeed." The Mouse Destroyer plucked up Prim's withered hand and gave it a little kiss. Prim snatched her hand away and glared at him, but Prude flushed pink with pleasure.

"May I ask your names, fair maidens?" the Baron asked.

"I'm Prudence, and this is Primrose," Prude twittered. Prim scowled and jabbed her in the side with the knitting needle.

"Delightful," the Baron said. "Now that we've met, I have a rather—er—delicate question to ask. I hate to ask it,

but I must. Do you"—he lowered his voice discreetly—"have a mouse problem?"

"A mouse problem?" Prim said. "Oh, no. Not at all."

"Of course we do!" Prude hissed, her bright hedge-hoggy eyes darting between Prim and the handsome Mouse Destroyer.

"Forgive me, ladies," the Baron said, "but I don't quite understand. Have you, or have you not, a mouse problem? I only ask because quite a few dead mice have been observed clogging the river downstream from here." He coughed. "The Department of Health has traced the mice to this location."

Prim let out a strangled cry as a mouse plummeted from a cobwebby chandelier and landed on her hat. Then she drew herself up to her full five feet of height. "Our house is very clean, thank you," she said. "No mice."

"Prim, the *Department of Health*!" Prude whispered urgently. "The *authorities*."

Prim ignored her and went on. "Now kindly remove yourself from our doorstep. This is private property, and we do not wish to be disturbed by trespassers."

"Even dashingly handsome ones?" Prude pleaded.

But the Mouse Destroyer wasn't listening to them at that point. He was staring down into the glittering black eyes of the mouse on Prim's hat. The mouse stared back.

"Listen to me," the Baron muttered, leaning so close

that his fabulous mustache twitched against Prim's forehead. "Listen to me, you rascal. I'm the Baron von Bilgeworth, Mouse Destroyer Extraordinaire, and darned if I haven't stomped hundreds of thousands of your rotten relatives. Are you listening, mouse? If you aren't trembling, you should be."

Anastasia, watching from her shadow, saw that the mouse *was* trembling. Anastasia was trembling, too. She was afraid for that mouse.

"Now, I'm not going to end your pathetic little life right this minute," the Baron went on, his voice soft. "I'm going to give you the chance of a lifetime, mouse. I'm actually going to help you to the floor, and then you're going to scamper back to your mouse brothers and sisters and tell them the Mouse Destroyer is here. I'm doing this because I like a challenge, not because I like you or any of your filthy friends. I like a challenge and so I'm giving you a head start. I'm going to count to one hundred, mouse, and then ready or not"—he grinned, showing strong white teeth—"here I come."

While he was talking, he reached up ever so slowly and then brought his hand down over the mouse and closed his fingers around it. Anastasia was gobsmacked. Why hadn't the mouse somersaulted out of reach? The old ladies were gobsmacked, too. Prude's mouth was hanging open, and she was gazing at the Baron in frank admiration.

"Down you go," the Baron said, bending down and

setting the mouse carefully on the floor. The mouse didn't move. It blinked at the Baron in a kind of daze.

"*One,*" the Baron said.

And the mouse zinged right out of the hall before he could utter *two.*

"How on earth did you do that?" Prude asked. "It's like the horrid thing could understand you!"

"Ladies, I've made a career out of mouse squashing," the Baron replied. "I've squelched millions of the little sods. It's my passion. It's my calling. I've chased mice from New Zealand to London to the Bronx. And believe me, that mouse *did* understand me."

"You said the Department of Health sent you?" Prim asked, her voice suspicious.

"No, no," the Baron replied. "The Department of Health traced the mouse infestation to this house. I have a friend who works there. Tom Sogwind. You may know him?"

The old ladies shook their heads.

"Well, Tommy knows about my talent, and he gave me a tip. The Department of Health is going to pay you a visit next week, unless you get your mouse problem under control." The Baron grimaced. "I can assure you, you don't want the Department of Health tromping around your lovely home. They're very—*ahem*—thorough. They rummage through all your most private places. They peer into every cupboard and closet. I've heard they even read diaries."

"Not our diaries!" Prude said.

"Now, I could help you out," the Baron said. "I would be glad to. And then you wouldn't have to deal with all those bothersome bureaucrats."

"The problem is," Prim said, "we can't pay you."

"We haven't any money," Prude explained sadly.

"Money!" the Baron echoed. "Money! Who said anything about money? I don't need *money*. I'm filthy rich as it is. What I need," he said, "is mouse blood. I'm like a tiger, ladies. A mouse-stalking tiger. Tigers don't expect to be *paid* for hunting, do they?"

And with his gleaming green eyes and ginger-colored whiskers, he did look rather like a fine tiger.

"I love the hunt," the Baron went on. "I offer my service free of charge." His smile went away, and his brow furrowed. "Perhaps I should explain *why* I despise mice so much," he said. "I wouldn't want you to think I'm some kind of nut. Let me tell you a little story from my military days. I used to have ten magnificent toes, ladies. Wonderfully masculine toes with perfectly square nails, and I trimmed them and cleaned them every single day after the marches."

"*Used* to have?" Prude said. "What happened to your magnificent toes?"

"Did you step on a land mine?" Prim asked, sneaking a look at the Baron's shiny boots.

"No, I did not," the Baron said. "I woke up one morning

to find that mice had chewed off my toes, each and every one."

Anastasia, who had never worried about that kind of problem, flexed her toes inside her galoshes. They all seemed to be accounted for.

"So you can understand why I hate mice, and why I devote my life to stomping them," he said darkly. "*Revenge*. Revenge is a delicious dish, ladies, and I like to eat often."

Prim slid the knitting needle into her coat pocket and said, "Won't you come in for a cup of tea?"

"I should be delighted to." And he tromped into the room, the soles of his glossy black boots squishing hundreds of little mouse droppings.

"You will forgive us," Prim said, "if we ask you to turn out your pockets and open your trunk."

"We're not in the habit of letting strangers in," Prude warbled.

"Forgive you?" the Baron said. "Why, I *admire* you. One can never be too cautious, I always say." He pulled the pockets of his trousers inside out so they dangled from his hips like cotton tongues. He unbuttoned his military jacket to display the silk lining. He even opened his mouth and said *Ahh*. The old ladies peered at his teeth, nodding appreciatively.

"Nice, aren't they?" he asked. "I'm particularly proud of my molars. And you'll find my tonsils are in order, too."

Then he set his trunk down with a thump and undid the clasps and flipped the lid up. "This, mesdemoiselles, is my Mouse Murdering Trunk."

"*Oooooooooh,*" breathed Prim and Prude.

Inside the suitcase was nothing more than a round, smooth yellow wheel of cheese the size of a small tire.

"Do you see this cheese?" he asked. "It looks rather delectable, doesn't it? It's very special, this cheese."

"It smells lovely," Prude sighed. "Is that Swiss?"

"Don't be a twit," Prim said. "Do you see any holes?"

"No," Prude admitted.

"Why is this cheese so special, Baron?" Prim asked.

"Because," the Mouse Destroyer said, snapping his trunk closed again, "we're going to use this beautiful lump of cheese to murder every single rotten mouse stinking up this house, or at least the ones I don't trounce before they get a nibble. Now, I believe you mentioned tea."

The kidnappers led the Baron off into the gloom of the asylum.

Murder the mice! It was disgusting! Anastasia quivered with the need to escape. And then she noticed that, in all the excitement of the arrival of the handsome Mouse Destroyer and his demonstration of mouse-intimidation techniques and the inspection of his molars and murderous cheese, the front door had been left slightly ajar.

She ran down the stairwell and out to the porch. She

couldn't leave right that moment, of course. She couldn't abandon Quentin and Ollie. But Anastasia had something else in mind.

She hotfooted it to the pink station wagon and flung open the driver's-side door. Her hand darted in and clamped over the gate opener. Her head swiveled toward the iron spikes of the electric fence.

"What the biscuit?" she muttered.

The Mouse Destroyer had strolled, supposedly, through the open front gates, but the fence ahead loomed as grim and locked as ever. She stared in puzzlement. And then she gave a little jump. The poodles had scented her and were galloping her way!

Lickety-split, Anastasia clambered back up the stairs and over the mirrored stoop and nicked into the asylum. The poodles prowled at the base of the front steps, twitching their

fuzzy lips and displaying their nasty metal chompers. Anastasia let out a woozy sigh of relief, shoving the gate opener into her coat pocket.

Then she raced through the hallways and tiptoed up the spiral staircase to the Watchtower. She peeked around the doorjamb.

The Baron was gazing at the asylum grounds. "Splendid bog you have there," he said before accepting a cup of tea from Prude and settling upon an ottoman. "Give me forty-eight hours, ladies. Forty-eight hours, and you won't have a single mouse left in this charming home. Not only that, but no mouse will ever again dare to darken your doorway."

"You sound very confident," Prim said.

"Oh, I am," the Baron said. "My mouse-stomping methods are foolproof. See these medals, girls?" He pointed to the buttons on his lapel. "I didn't survive the war on sheer good looks alone. I had to be cunning. I had to be quick. And even though I left the military after the war, I never stopped fighting. Now my war is on mice." He swigged his tea in one great swallow. Then he stood up, stroking his mustache and pacing the tower like the mouse-hunting tiger he was. "Forty-eight hours. Are you with me, ladies?"

Prude's hopeful eyes stared into Prim's cloudy blue ones. Prim sighed and nodded.

"Excellent." The Baron grinned at them and sat down again. His voice became warm and conversational. "So, what are two pretty girls like you doing all by yourselves in this great big house?"

The Watchers exchanged another look.

"We aren't exactly alone," Prude said.

"No?"

"Well," Prude said reluctantly, "aside from a gardener with biting madness, we do have a little girl living here."

"A niece," said Prim.

"A niece, eh? Well, tell her to stay clear of me. I hate mouse pests and I hate pesky children. Actually . . ." The Baron stroked his chin. "Perhaps I could use her help. A little girl could squeeze into small places to set out the Liquid Death. It's powerful stuff. Burns right through the skin."

Anastasia's freckly hide tingled just hearing about it. *Liquid Death?*

"I'm sure she'll be happy to help you," Prim said.

"I don't care whether she's happy about it or not," the Baron said, extracting a small square of lace from his vest pocket and blotting his mustache with it. "I'm ready for battle. Let's go meet this nauseating little niece of yours, shall we?"

23

The Black Envelope

ANASTASIA FLEW DOWN the tower stairs and galoshed through the corridors to the Great Hall, not even stopping to catch her breath before pounding up the front staircase. She was, after all, supposed to be in her room. Most unfortunately, she slipped on a patch of mold fuzzing the third step from the top and slid all the way back down to the bottom, sprawling painfully in the dust just as Prim and Prude and the Mouse Destroyer rounded the corner.

"Is this more of your yoga nonsense?" Prude cried. "Stand up and meet the Baron von Bilgeworth. He's here to help us with our mouse problem."

"And *you* are going to help him," said Prim.

"I shall call her," the Baron declared, stroking his mustache, "Reginald."

"Reginald?" Prim echoed.

"Reginald," he said. "That was the name of one of my sergeants back in the war. Just like you, he had millions of nasty little freckles."

"I don't have millions," Anastasia said hoarsely. "I've got exactly one hundred twenty-seven."

"But that isn't why you remind me of him. Do you know why I remember Reginald after all these years?"

Anastasia was so frightened that she could only let out a little squeak.

"I remember him," the Baron said, "because I shot him in the back as he was running away. I don't like cowards."

"Oh," Anastasia yawped. She staggered to her feet.

The Baron dropped his Mouse Murdering Trunk in front of her, almost squashing her ten intact toes. "Now," he announced, "it's time to cook up the Liquid Death." He turned to Prim and Prude with a charming smile. "Reginald and I have lots of preparations to make, and most of them are rather unpleasant. You two should run along and do whatever it is attractive and fun-loving ladies enjoy doing, and Reggie and I will get started with our work."

"Can't we help you with anything?" Prude asked.

"Just show us to the kitchen," the Baron replied cheerfully. "And once we're in there, I'd advise you to stay out. Liquid Death fumes are pretty toxic. I've built up a tolerance, but I wouldn't be surprised if every last strand of Reginald's hair fell out by morning."

Not three minutes later, Prim and Prude were back up in their glass tower, and Anastasia was left alone with the Mouse Destroyer beneath the pointy tips of the knives dangling from the kitchen ceiling. She stared at the floor tiles. She swallowed hard.

"It's wrong to hurt animals," she said. "It's despicable. You're bigger than me and maybe I can't stop you from doing whatever awful thing you're about to do, but I'm not going to help you. And I don't care what you do to me."

This last part was, of course, a whopping great lie. She cared very much what fate awaited her at the hands of the Baron von Bilgeworth. She was scared silly.

"Anastasia," the Baron said softly.

Her head snapped up.

The Mouse Destroyer was studying her carefully. "You poor child." His voice was quiet and gentle, and his face was gentle, too. "Those two crab apples have been treating you very badly, haven't they?"

Anastasia hadn't known what exactly to expect from the Mouse Destroyer, but it certainly hadn't been that. She gazed at him in utter bewilderment.

"They're monsters," the Baron went on. "Absolutely mean old meanies." And then a really astonishing thing happened.

His eyes grew very, very shiny, and then tears began slipping down his cheeks until his beautiful mustache was soggy. He sat down on his Mouse Murdering Trunk. Now his shining green eyes were level with Anastasia's round brown ones.

"My dear girl," the Baron said, "please forgive me for saying all those terrible things just a minute ago. But you see, I had to do it. I had to convince those crab apples that I could do their dirty job of mouse murdering. It was the only way to get into the house."

"How," Anastasia said slowly, "did you know my name?"

"You must forget all those things that I said," the Baron went on. "Let me promise you that I have *never* squashed a mouse. Can you believe me? Can you?"

Now, you can probably understand that Anastasia might have been an eensie bit skeptical. Primrose and Prudence, for example, seemed like two pink-cheeked specimens of sweet-little-old-ladyhood, but they were, in fact, two mouse-hating, child-snatching murderers. If Anastasia had never trusted anyone again, it would be sad but completely understandable.

But, dear Reader, here is the interesting and inspiring thing: she *did* believe the Baron von Bilgeworth. Looking at him now, she knew that he would never hurt anyone small and innocent, whether furry mouse or stinky kid. "I believe you," she said.

He smiled at her. Then he took out his lace hankie and blotted his eyes and mustache. "Listen," he said, "we have to get you out of here. This loony bin is no place for a child."

Anastasia nodded vigorously.

"We can't leave just now," the Baron said. "We have to wait until tonight. In the meantime, we must keep up the charade that I am a cruel mouse exterminator, or those two nasty prunes will send me away and you'll be left all alone with them again."

Technically, Anastasia reasoned, she wouldn't be all alone. She would have Ollie and Quentin. But beholding the strong and kind man before her, she felt much better about all the holes in the Beastly Dreadfuls' escape plan.

The Baron broke into her thoughts. "In fact, they might be wondering why they can't hear any shouting or smacking or general mouse murdering. So let's give them a little show, shall we?" His eyes were now gleaming with mischief and merriment. He unhooked his riding crop from his belt and slammed it down on the countertop with a *CRASH.* "You toe-chewing scum!" he bellowed at the top of his lungs. "You fur-covered menace! Die, worm-tailed rotter! Death to mice!"

Of course, the Baron was not actually assaulting any mice. He wasn't even touching them. A group of about twenty mice watched from a stack of dishes piled in the sink, their eyes bright and curious. But Prim and Prude heard the thumping and screaming all the way up in their glass tower. They smiled nastily at each other and continued to knit.

"A pox on rodents!" the Baron shouted.

Then he sat down on the trunk again and held his hand out flat with the palm up. He made a noise in the back of his manly throat, and one of the mice galloped across the floor and leapt right into his hand.

"Well done, you," the Baron said to it.

The mouse squeaked.

"Good, good," the Baron said. "I was worried, of course." He stroked the mouse's back with his index finger, and the mouse closed its eyes and sighed.

"Can that mouse actually understand you?" Anastasia yelped.

"Indeed she can," the Baron said.

"But how? Are these mice your—your pets or something?" Anastasia had once read a story about a circus of performing mice. The ringleader had trained each and every mouse to do wonderful things like riding tiny unicycles and squeaking Christmas carols.

"These mice and I know each other very well," the Baron said. "Let's just say that this mouse infiltration was a joint effort."

"*You* let the mice loose in the house?"

"Something like that. Now," he went on, "we'll leave tonight."

"But, Mr. von Bilgeworth," Anastasia said, "why did you even come here in the first place? If you aren't a Mouse Destroyer, why exactly are you here?"

He looked very grave. The mouse flipped onto its back, and the Baron tickled its tummy. "Because I knew you were here, Anastasia," he said. "I came to help you escape."

She mulled this over. It sounded extraordinary, but it

didn't *feel* extraordinary. Somehow it made sense. Whereas it had felt totally *wrong* when Prim and Prude had lured her from Mooselick Elementary, it felt weirdly *right* that the Baron von Bilgeworth and his army of mice had arrived at St. Agony's Asylum to help her.

"How did you know I was here?" Her heart thumped a hopeful little tattoo. "Did my parents send you? Are you some kind of detective?"

The Baron shook his head. "No, child," he said. "Your parents didn't send me, and I'm not a detective. Although I do enjoy detective stories."

"But how do you know who I am?"

His green eyes twinkled at her. "We've been looking for you," he said, "ever since the moment those two nasty prunes whisked you away from Mooselick Elementary. We tracked you to this dreary pile of bricks."

"*We?*" Anastasia echoed. "You and the mice?"

"Miss Apple and I," the Baron said.

"You mean the librarian at my school?" Anastasia gave a little jump. "You *know* Miss Apple?" The idea that the dashing Baron was somehow acquainted with the meek little librarian was shocking.

"I do indeed," the Baron told her. "In fact, I have in my possession a letter for you from Miss Apple." He put the mouse on his shoulder. He stooped down to unsnap the brass buckles of his Mouse Murdering Trunk and hoisted the cheese wheel out. He plucked a knife from the ceiling and sawed the wheel right down the middle. The mice watched with bright interest, their pink nostrils quivering in the air. Anastasia gasped as a little black envelope popped out of one of the cheese halves and fell onto the floor.

"The wheel is hollow," the Baron whispered. "It was made by a friend of mine, an expert cheese monger."

Anastasia stooped to pick up the curious black envelope. Miss Apple's neat librarian cursive curled across the front in gold ink.

Anastasia tilted the envelope, watching the ink glimmer in the fading light from the dusty window, and then she turned the envelope over. It was sealed with a big gob of blue-violet wax squished down on the flap. She had never seen anything like it, and the fact that such a fancy letter came from practical, mousy Miss Apple was bewildering indeed.

"Go ahead," the Baron said. "Open it."

❦ 24 ❦
The Great Cheese Caper

Dear Anastasia,

There is no time to waste. You must trust Mr. Baron von Bilgeworth. He will help you escape that unsanitary mansion and take you to a safe place. He is an ally (that is, a friend), and you can trust him completely.

I'm so sorry for the hardship you have endured. When we next see each other (soon!), I will bring some lovely books for you. Did you know there is a new Francie Dewdrop mystery? It's titled The Clue in the Foggy Forest. And the December issue of Learning Is Fun includes a most wonderful article about pus. Did you know that pus is actually white blood cells? And—

Well, we can chat about pus later. For now, you are in Grave Peril (that is, terrible danger) and must flee

*St. Agony's Asylum as soon as possible. Destroy this letter
after you have finished reading it. Please don't try to burn it,
though, because that would be a fire hazard.*

Sincerely,

Miss Apple

It was from Miss Apple, all right. Nobody else would
deem an article about pus "most wonderful."

"It says I should destroy this letter after reading it," she
told the Baron.

"Eat it," he urged.

"Eat it?" Anastasia protested. "Ugh!"

"In that case," the Baron said, "I suppose we can just
tear it up." And he plucked the letter from her hands and
shredded it into confetti and tossed it over the mice. He said,
"Huzzah!" The mice stared at him.

"Miss Apple suspected something was wrong when she
noticed Miss Sneed dragging you down the hall," the Baron
went on.

"That's right," Anastasia said slowly, thinking back to
that fateful day at Mooselick Elementary. "I saw her watching us."

"And when she saw that pink station wagon peeling
out of the parking lot with you stuck in the back, she just
knew you had fallen into the clutches of those miserable
kidnappers."

"So you know about the other children?" Anastasia exclaimed. "You know Prim and Prude are awful child-snatchers?"

"Indeed I do," the Baron said. "They're scoundrels. They're scum of the earth." He whacked his crop against the pots and pans dangling from the ceiling. "SCUM OF THE EARTH! SCUM OF THE EARTH!" The mouse clung to his collar, tail swinging.

"Shhh!" Anastasia hissed. "They'll hear you!"

"That's all right. They'll just think I'm shouting at the mice," the Baron said. "But sometimes I can't control myself when I think about those treacherous child-snatchers. Foul! Horrible! NASTY AS WORM POO!"

Up in the Watchtower, Prude commented, "This fellow really knows his stuff. Those mice must be shaking in their boots."

"Mice don't wear boots, Prudence," Prim replied.

"SICKENING, REVOLTING, SCUM OF THE SOLAR SYSTEM!" the Baron bellowed, replacing the riding switch to his belt. "Whew! Now I feel a bit better. Anyway, as you have already deduced, those two old prunes have snatched all sorts of children. They're seasoned old villains. I don't want to frighten you, Anastasia, but Prude and Prim"—he glanced around warily, then continued in a low murmur—"will kill you if they deem it necessary."

Anastasia, who had already known this for days, nonetheless felt a pinch of fear between her shoulder blades.

"They would use your guts for Christmas garland," the Baron went on. "That's why we have to be ever so careful when we escape. It isn't just a matter of sauntering out the front door of this moldering mansion. Oh, no! They'd try to kill us on the spot. And while I've tangled with the likes of Prim and Prude before, it would be much better for us to sneak away unnoticed. Hopefully, we'll be miles away by the time they realize we're gone."

Anastasia nodded. The League of Beastly Dreadfuls had already drawn the same conclusion. She wondered whether she should tell the Baron about Quentin and Ollie. She *wanted* to. Miss Apple's letter said, *You can trust him completely.* But Quentin and Ollie were Shadowfolk, and she was pinkie-sworn not to spill their top-secret beans.

"Tell me," the Baron said, "do they lock you into your room?"

Anastasia nodded again. "Every night at sundown."

The Baron rubbed his chin. "I wonder if there's a skeleton key around this old dump. Or I could try picking the lock. That always works for Francie Dewdrop, although I've never actually done it myself."

"You read Francie Dewdrop?" Anastasia exclaimed.

"Of course I do," the Baron said with great dignity.

"Wonderful stories. She's a first-rate detective-veterinarian-artist. So brave and clever, and all those lovely illustrations. My favorite story is number thirteen, *The Conundrum at Mildew Manor.* That's the one with the skeleton key," he added.

"Actually, Mr. Bilgeworth, we don't need a skeleton key," Anastasia said. "And we won't have to pick the lock. I *made* a key."

And she summarized the triumph of the Choco-Laxative and her delicious sugar key, careful to leave out mention of Ollie and Quentin's help. She felt a little guilty taking all the credit for the combined efforts of the League of Beastly Dreadfuls, but she had to keep the Shadowboys' existence mum.

"Ingenious!" the Baron raved. "You clever child! My hat goes off to you! Well, I don't actually have a hat, but you know what I mean. Now, back to our escape. Let's consider the obstacles."

"The poodles," Anastasia said grimly.

"Ah, yes," the Baron said. "The guard poodles. They are a problem, aren't they?" He shuddered. "Please don't ever repeat this to anyone, but I have a bit of a . . . fear of poodles. I'm poodlephobic. I'm ashamed of it, but the fact is they scare the living daylights out of me. Even teacup poodles."

"Really?"

"Oh, gosh, yes," the Baron said. "Frightful animals."

The kitchen was silent as they both pondered the problem of poodles.

"I have an idea," Anastasia spoke up. "If you aren't really going to poison the mice, you won't need this cheese wheel, will you?"

"No," the Baron said. "That cheese was for smuggling secret letters, not mouse murdering."

Anastasia unbuttoned her satchel, pulled out a small bottle, and presented it to the Baron.

"Dr. Bluster's Patented Sleep Preparation of Most Sleepful Sleep!" he said. "I've heard of this stuff! It's supposed to be strong enough to knock a rhino on its . . . er. Well."

"This is what Prim and Prude use to drug children when they go snatching," Anastasia said angrily. "They used it on me. And I was planning to give them a dose of their own medicine! But now I have a different idea. We'll paint the cheese with this sleeping potion and give it to the poodles. They love cheese. They can't resist it."

"Anastasia, you amaze me!" the Baron cried. "What a grand idea!"

"Let's just make sure the kidnappers are still up in their Watchtower," Anastasia whispered. "I wouldn't want them to catch us with this stuff." She crept over to the speaking tube, and she and the Baron both leaned close to the silver trumpet.

"Primrose?"

"Yes?"

"Don't you just adore the Baron's mustache? It's so handsome. So *manly*."

"Prudence, you sap, of *course* his mustache is manly! It's a *mustache*!"

"Wouldn't he look fine with a monobrow?" Prude asked.

"Prudence, my word!" Prim snorted. "You are the silliest fool when it comes to men. You're man-mad, you are!"

"I am not!"

"You most certainly *are*. My goodness, I'll never forget how you used to moon over that foot doctor. You were giddier than a sixteen-year-old on prom night every time you sprouted a new bunion!"

"Shut up, Primrose!"

"And I'm certain you faked that case of athlete's foot just for an excuse to talk to him!"

Anastasia dropped the speaking tube, and she and the Baron howled with laughter for a few minutes. Then they returned to the serious business of plotting the great cheese caper. Anastasia took out her dinky paintbrush and dipped it into the bottle, then started painting the cheese.

"Is there enough of that stuff to slip some into the kidnappers' tea?" the Baron asked. "That could really help us along."

Anastasia peered into the bottle. "It looks like there's only enough in here for the cheese. There wasn't much to begin with."

"Think of all the children they've drugged with their diabolical peppermints," the Baron growled. "THE SCUM!

Oh, well. We'll get past them tonight. I'll throw the cheese to the poodles when those nasty kidnappers lock you in your room at sundown. Just don't expect me to get too close to those fluffy terrors." He shuddered again.

Once the cheese was painted, the Baron replaced it in the trunk and shut the lid. Several of the mice squeaked their disappointment.

"That cheese is strictly off-limits," the Baron admonished them, fastening the buckles.

"Obstacle number two: Prim and Prude," Anastasia said. "Now that we don't have the sleeping stuff to zonk them, what are we going to do?"

The Baron furrowed his handsome forehead. He stroked his mustache.

Anastasia stared at him. His mustache *was* manly, just like Prude said. He looked a little bit—actually, *quite* a bit—like the strapping fellow on the cover of Prude's book *The Handsome Rogue Who Fell in Love with the Older Lady*.

"I have an idea," she said. "I know Prude's weakness."

Knowing your enemy's weakness, dear Reader, is one of the crucial tenets of the art of war.

"Really? What?" The Baron snapped out of his reverie.

"You," Anastasia said.

"*Me?*"

"Yes, you," Anastasia said. "Prude is man-mad. *And* she likes your mustache. You heard it yourself."

"Elderly child-murderers aren't really my type," the Baron objected.

"But Prude's the one on guard tonight, and I bet you could distract her while we—I mean, while *I* sneak out to the back garden."

The Baron pondered this. "I suppose I could ask her about those bunions," he mused. He clenched his magnificent jaw. "You're right; that's our best bet. I'll summon up every last bit of my manly charm to fool Prude into neglecting her guard duties."

"I don't think it will be terribly difficult," Anastasia said. "You're very charming."

A pleased blush crept into the Baron's cheeks. "Well," he murmured, "I don't wish to boast, but my mustache *is* rather glorious."

"Exactly." Anastasia did a happy little tap dance. It seemed like the Beastly Dreadfuls' great escape was really coming together. The poodles would be snoozing, and Prude would swoon beneath the spell of the Baron's facial hair. And once they got through the fence, Ollie and Quentin could buzz back home, and the Baron would whisk Anastasia back to Mooselick.

"All right," the Baron said. "I'll massage Prude's bunions, if that's what it takes to keep her out of the Watchtower while you pussyfoot it out to the garden. But how are we going to get you out of this nuthouse? I noticed a tricky combination lock on the front door."

"It was designed by a master locksmith," Anastasia said. "But don't worry. I have another way out. A—um—a secret passageway." She didn't want to reveal the Beastly Dreadfuls' real exit route. She had a feeling the Baron would declare it too dangerous.

"Secret passageway?" the Baron marveled. "My gosh, this place is the Four Seasons of spooky old insane asylums! Five stars! Now, once you're in the topiary grove, hide behind a bush and wait for me."

"Thank you for coming to help me," Anastasia said. "But why did you, again?"

"DIE, WRETCHED CANKER ON THE BUTTOCK OF HUMANITY!" the Baron thundered for the kidnappers' benefit. To Anastasia he said, "Miss Apple and I have been watching you for many years. Our main priority is your safety and protection."

"But *why*?" Anastasia asked, more puzzled than ever. "I'm not rich or important or special. I'm just a normal kid.

Even," she mumbled, taking into consideration her freckles and flatulence, "a slightly below-average kid."

"Ah, but that is where you are wrong, Anastasia," the Baron said quietly. "You are *very* special. You see—"

At that moment, the door swung open, and Prim and Prude stuck their fluffy heads into the kitchen.

"How's the murdering going?" Prude asked.

"Splendidly," the Baron boasted. "Behold my vanquished enemies."

Anastasia, like the old child-snatchers, looked down at the floor. Dozens of mice lay on their backs with their pink toes sticking in the air.

"How wonderful!" chirped Prude. "It looks like you've been very busy."

"I have been," the Baron said. "I've killed quite a few of the nasty rotters."

"It seems a shame to interrupt your good work," Prim said, "but Nice Little Girls must be in bed before dark, you know."

Anastasia glanced at the Baron. His eyes were hard as glass. "Run along, Reginald," he said coolly. "May you dream of dead mice."

❧ 25 ❧

Into the Mercurial Garden

ANASTASIA WAITED UNTIL the kidnappers clunked the chain on the other side of the door to Room Eleven. Then she sprang into action. She flung open the doors of her wardrobe, dredging out Mr. Bunster and looking him straight in the eye.

"This is it, Mr. Bunster," she said. "The night of our big escape. The Great Cheese Caper. The Daring Escape of the League of Beastly Dreadfuls."

Mr. Bunster's black button glinted.

"Be brave," she told him. "Even little rabbits must be brave." She shoved him down into her satchel, cushioning Ollie's music box. She froze, her hand still jammed in the bag. Thinking very hard, she pulled out her sketch pad and ripped one corner from the tear-streaked portrait of Fred

McCrumpet. Her pencil was just a stub, but she managed to scratch a few words onto the scrap. Then she folded it into a tiny origami frog. She put the frog at the edge of the wood shelf at the bottom of the wardrobe and pressed his rear end down. The paper amphibian tiddlywinked into the wardrobe's lightless depths, and she closed the doors after him.

Reader, if you ever find yourself in a gloomy Victorian insane asylum surrounded by a forest of dark trees, and you happen to discover an origami frog in the wardrobe of Room Eleven, go ahead and unfold it. There's a note written inside. The note will tell you that the two sweet old ladies knitting in the glass tower upstairs are plotting to add your bones to their garden, so you should start planning your escape. Keep your eyes peeled for just such a note, Reader! It could prove the difference between life and death.

Anastasia stared at Mr. McCrumpet's portrait for a moment, brimming with hope. Perhaps she would even be back in Mooselick in time for a big McCrumpet waffle breakfast! She replaced the picture in her satchel and checked her watch.

It was time to act.

She rummaged in her pocket for the most splendiferous jawbreaker in confectionary history. The sugar key sparkled in her hand like something magical. Click. Click. *Clunk.* Anastasia slid the magnet across the door until she heard the telltale thunk. She laid her hand on the doorknob.

It was cold and smooth beneath her clammy palm. Her heart was beating so hard that she could feel her pulse throbbing where her skin pressed against the metal. It was easy to imagine that she was actually feeling the house's heartbeat. She thought of that second night in the asylum, cradled in the child-shaped hollow of her cot and crying for her dead parents and fancying that the house wept with her, too.

She shook the memory away and opened the door.

She locked it behind her and pulled the chain back through its metal track. She scrunched her eyes, waiting for her pupils to drink in the dim light in the corridor. She couldn't, of course, carry a candle through the mansion as she made her escape. Fortunately, after all the weeks of creeping through the nooks and crannies and armpits of the ancient asylum, it seemed like her eyeballs were adapting to darkness.

"Am I glad to see you!" Ollie piped up.

Anastasia started. *"Shhhh!"* she hissed. "Ollie, we have to be quiet." She let out a deep breath. "Crumbs, you surprised me! I can't see you at all."

"Anastasia? I'm still worried about the poodles," Ollie said. "I'm actually not sure I could bite a poodle. I *like* dogs, even vicious guard poodles."

"Never mind that," Anastasia said. "We have to go. Remember, *escape or die trying.* That's the credo of the Beastly Dreadfuls."

"Right!" Ollie said. "Escape or die! Goody!"

They zigzagged through the asylum to Room Thirty-Eight.

"Knock, knock," Ollie whispered.

Quentin pulled off his head cage and threw it on the carpet. "Anastasia, did you drug Prim and Prude?"

"No," Anastasia said. "We drugged the poodles instead."

"We?" the Shadowboys echoed.

"The Baron and I," Anastasia said.

"The Baron?"

"He came to help us—I mean, me—escape. We smeared Dr. Bluster's sleeping stuff on some cheese, and the Baron threw it to the poodles while Prim and Prude were locking me in my room."

"Can we trust him?" Quentin demanded. "What if he's another kidnapper? What if he's . . . *Uncle Snodgrass?*"

"He isn't," Anastasia assured him. "He's friends with Miss Apple, the librarian at my elementary school. And we can trust him completely."

"Did you tell him about Ollie and me?"

"No," Anastasia said, fumbling in her pocket for her quarter. "He doesn't know. And right now he's busy distracting Prude, so we have to leave. Lefty loosey. Lefty loosey. Lefty loosey." She heaved the mirror away from the doorway. "Ready?"

"Ready," Quentin said. Then his ragged frocks crumpled to a heap, and his skinny shadow rippled across the rug. Anastasia couldn't even see Ollie and Quentin as they slinked together down the gloomy stairwell, but she could hear Ollie humming "Ballad of the Lovelorn Beluga."

"Ollie, be *quiet*. We're escaping. *Crumbs!*" Anastasia squelched a yelp as her toe nudged against something. She looked down.

It was one of the Baron's mice, lying on his back with his toes pointing in the air. Her heart sank.

"Is it dead?" Ollie whispered.

"I don't know."

Had the mouse stumbled into one of Prim and Prude's murderous traps? She hunched down and carefully picked the mouse up. His body was warm. She could feel his tiny mouse heart thrumming inside his furry chest. But his eyes were squinched closed.

"He's alive," she said. "Maybe he fainted."

"Perhaps he suffers from low blood pressure," Quentin said. "I know a tuba player who always passes out during his solo in 'Dance of the Flatulent Fairy.' Very awkward."

"He should switch to the triangle," Ollie suggested.

Anastasia put the mouse into her coat pocket, and they continued down the hallway.

Was that . . . *another* mouse?

Anastasia frowned and stooped down. She poked the mouse with her finger. Its hind paws twitched, and it let out a sputtery squeak.

"Was that a *snore*?" Ollie asked.

Anastasia nodded grimly. "A *cheesy* snore."

And now that her eyeballs had fully adjusted to the murky asylum, she could see dozens of furry little blobs dotting the rose-colored carpet. She pocketed the snoring mouse and picked up the next one, and the next, examining them.

Sure enough, every single mouse was sound asleep.

It didn't take a brilliant detective-veterinarian-artist to deduce that the mice had gotten into the crumbs of cheese left behind by the poodles.

"We can't just leave them lying around," Anastasia said. "What if the kidnappers find them?"

She hopscotched from mouse to mouse, carefully pocketing each one. A chorus of faint snores rustled from her coat as the Beastly Dreadfuls headed down the staircase to the Great Hall. Anastasia cast one last glance at the monobrowed ladies glaring from their portraits. "Goodbye, Viola Snodgrass." She shivered, thinking about returning to Mooselick Elementary, where the evil eyeball glinted from Miss Sneed's meaty pinkie. She would have to tell Miss Apple about Miss Sneed when she saw her. She thought back to the librarian's letter—*When we next see each other (soon!)*—and mentally hugged the words.

Thud. Thud.

"It's Prude!" Quentin said.

Anastasia snatched one last mouse from the bottom stair as the League invaded the Great Hall. She scrooched behind the sheet-shrouded harpsichord. She was just congratulating herself on her Francie Dewdroppy stealth when she banged her arm against the harpsichord's flank. *Zzzzznnng!*

The twin silver moons of Prude's eyeglasses swerved toward the harpsichord. Anastasia held her breath. She felt a chilly rustle and swiveled her eyeballs down to her body. The Shadowboys pressed against her, camouflaging her in the gloom. She hadn't expected them to be so *cold*. A mouse kicked in her satchel, squeaking in its sleep.

"Stupid vermin," Prude muttered. "You'll all be dead soon."

"Miss Prudence!" the Baron called, dashing into the Great Hall. "Oh, there you are. Did you find your book? It sounds so"—he flinched—"enticing."

"Here it is," Prude twittered, plucking a paperback off a sheeted whatnot. "I'm always leaving things scattered around. Silly me!"

"Will you read it aloud to me?" the Baron asked. "Your

voice is so soothing. You should narrate audiobooks. They'd sell like hotcakes."

Prude giggled. "We'll skip ahead to chapter seven. That's a particularly sizzling section."

"I *adore* sizzling literature," the Baron said.

As soon as Prude and the Baron had retreated, the Beastly Dreadfuls skirted between the credenzas and divans and davenports. All the way, Anastasia stooped and reached and crawled to pick up conked-out mice. It was like a fuzzy Easter egg hunt. When her bag was bursting with the Baron's whiskered comrades, she tiptoed into the small parlor off the Great Hall.

"All right." Anastasia stopped in front of the cobwebbed hearth. "Up we go. You first, Ollie."

"Pah!" Ollie's complaints echoed from inside the chimney. "It's filthy!"

Anastasia took a deep breath, then ducked into the fireplace's moonlit maw and grasped the first rung of the chimney sweep's ladder. It was rusty and cold, but it held her weight. She squeezed up, her fur coat rattling soot from the sides of the flue. Up, up, up, she went.

She popped her head out of the chimney.

"It's snowing," Ollie said, his boy-shape outlined against a moon-rimed gable.

Snowflakes wandered from the sky and tingled on Anastasia's pink face. She clambered up the final rungs and heaved herself out of the flue. Hugging the chimney, she gazed over the asylum grounds. Silver snow clouds snuffed out the stars, but the moon frosted the world with its phantasmagorical glow. It was the first time she had seen the asylum gardens at night, and they looked mercurial and magical in the dark and the moonlight and the snow. The scruffy topiaries seemed to shift and breathe as shadows fluttered over their leaves.

"That chimney *is* filthy." Quentin coughed, joining them on the roof. "Oh, the moon! The beautiful, wonderful, luminous, and lovely moon!"

Anastasia unwound Ollie's silky shadow legging from her neck and looped it around the chimney, cinching a sturdy knot. Clutching the end with both hands, she sat down and slowly tobogganed to the edge of the roof.

"Hold tight and don't let go," Quentin encouraged her. "We're right here beside you."

"Yes, but gravity isn't a problem for *you*," Anastasia said.

"Pretend you're the prince in Rapunzel," Ollie said.

"Ollie, you really need to brush up on your fairy tales," Anastasia said, eyeing the topiaries hulked below. "The prince falls onto rosebushes and goes blind."

"But everything worked out in the end," Quentin said. "Come on, Anastasia. You've got to jump!"

Anastasia swallowed. She stared at her green galoshes, swinging above the ground some twenty feet below. Then she swiveled her hips and shifted her weight so that she was dangling halfway off the gingerbreaded eave.

"If you die," Ollie reassured her, "we'll tell everyone that you were very brave."

Anastasia pumped her legs once, twice, three times, and then pushed off with her elbows and rappelled backward. *Zinnnnnng!* For a split second she was in free fall. Her stomach zoomed into her throat, and she clamped her teeth tight over a scream. Then the Shadowsilk stretched to its limit, and like a bungee jumper at the end of a gutsy leap, Anastasia rebounded slightly. She yo-yoed for several nauseating moments a few feet above the ground, and then she unclenched her hands and flopped back into the snow. The Shadowsilk snapped up the roof, shrinking back into a sock.

"You made it!" Ollie said beside her.

She staggered to her feet, and the Beastly Dreadfuls beelined to the back gardens. Anastasia's mouse-full pockets swung against her legs, and her mouse-stuffed satchel hung from her shoulder like lead. Her breath sparkled from her mouth and nostrils in icy little clouds as she huffed and puffed along the width of the asylum, until they came to the end of the stony wall.

"Do you see the poodles?" Quentin asked.

"No," Anastasia said. "They must be sleeping somewhere."

This was, quite possibly, the most dangerous part of the

entire escape. They would have to venture out into the garden, exposed. Even the Shadowboys would show up against the moonlit snow. If Prude happened to spy them from a window, they would lose any chance of a head start. Anastasia crouched like a racer waiting for the gunshot, her fingertips pressed against the cold ground.

Ready! Set! Go! To the nearest topiary, a blob that might have once been a lemur (or perhaps a raccoon)! Then to the wallaby (or enormous mouse)! To the monkey (or opossum)! She raced from bush to bush. Ollie and Quentin flitted along the frost beside her like dark snow angels until clouds blotted out the moon, and they disappeared into the gloom.

Anastasia squinted at a cluster of topiaries ahead. She again marveled at how different the garden looked at night, as though the bushes had shifted around in a game of musical chairs. It was easy, in that alchemical darkness, to imagine that the shrubberies yanked their roots from the cold earth and roamed the garden after sunset, playing their secret games until daybreak.

She bolted toward the grove and hunkered down by the closest bush.

The clouds peeled away from the moon.

The sound of her own panting filled Anastasia's ears. She glanced back at the asylum, its windows silvered by the moonlight and glinting like hundreds of unblinking peepers.

"It's like it's *watching* us," Ollie whispered.

Wheezing, Anastasia closed her eyes and slumped against the bush. It was surprisingly warm and soft.

One might even say cuddly.

And then she heard the noise.

She could even *feel* it. It buzzed inside her body. It was a low, low growl, and it was very near. Her eyelids snapped open. The growl swelled. Very, very slowly, she swiveled her eyeballs toward the rumble.

The topiary bush loomed over her. But it wasn't a bush, Anastasia saw with a shock. Not a bush at all! It was one of the poodles. Its eyes shone like nefarious fireflies. Its collar was thick as a man's belt and studded with long silver spikes. Its name tag flashed: SNOOKUMS. Snookums's purple lip curled up toward his nose, revealing a row of metal teeth.

"Oh, no," Ollie yipped beside her.

Anastasia stumbled backward. Too late, she realized that the nearest topiary bushes were, in fact, the well-trained and meticulously groomed attack poodles. Poodles are very intelligent animals, and these poodles were quite possibly criminal geniuses. They had pretended to be lawn shrubs. Their fluffy forms had blended into the garden of moonlight and shadow. Now each shadowy bush gleamed with eyes. The poodles inched nearer, champing their glittering jaws.

Anastasia was surrounded.

❧ 26 ❧
The Creature in the Woods

THE MICE, ANASTASIA concluded with an awful sinking feeling, hadn't just nibbled the *crumbs* of cheese left behind by the dogs. They had eaten it *all*! They had devoured the cheese before any of the fearsome guard poodles could take a single bite, and now those poodles were wide-awake and *very* disgruntled.

Snookums snarled.

"Nice doggy," Anastasia whispered.

He sprang.

Anastasia braced herself for the cataclysmic impact of claws and jaws and metal spikes against her tender almost-eleven-year-old skeleton. She closed her eyes. She gritted her teeth. She waited. In films, people on the verge of dying often glimpse a mishmash of memories. This is called *seeing your life flashing before your eyes,* and it's supposed to be like a little movie of important personal moments. Anastasia hoped she'd get to relive the day she won the Mooselick Elementary Bookworm Contest. Or it might be nice, she thought, to peep Muffy's grumpy little face one last time, or Mr. McCrumpet frowning at one of his dead plants, or Miss Apple smiling at a particularly thrilling article about lice or mold or some other scientific thing, or to hear Quentin's wobbly saw music, or Ollie laughing at silly limericks. And even though she had just met the dashing Baron von Bilgeworth, Anastasia would have liked to see him again, too. But Anastasia didn't see anything at all.

"Oooof!" Cold jozzled her bones, sending her sprawling to the ground. Her eyelashes stuttered open in time to see Snookums skidding across the ice a few feet away, silver chops crunching down onto thin air.

She peered at the chilly gloom plastering her coat. "Quentin?"

The Shadowboy unspooled from her, panting. "That was close! He missed us by a whisker!"

"First-rate belly flop!" Ollie applauded. "Ten out of ten!"

Anastasia wheeled her gaze back to Snookums. The villain was scooting in reverse on his haunches, toenails skittering, a frightened whine rattling his metal teeth. The other poodles were also backing away from the Beastly Dreadfuls, chorusing with whimpers.

"They're *scared* of you!" Anastasia exclaimed.

"No," Ollie said in a tiny voice. "They're scared of *that*."

Anastasia crooked her chin over her shoulder. A wolf—a huge, brown *wolf*—crouched amidst the topiaries, its muzzle tight around its fangs. Anastasia squeaked as the wolf let out a bellow. Her mind reeled. *It must be the Creature!*

She scrambled to a topiary shaped like a giraffe (or brachiosaur) and shrank against its leaves. Ollie and Quentin furled their shadowy forms over her.

AWOOOOOOOO! The wolf lunged toward the pack of poodles. *AWOOOOOOOO!* The becurled canines turned tail and galloped into the night, barking like mad. The wolf dashed after them, hot on their fluffy heels.

Anastasia tore her gaze away from the chase and strained her eyes into the darkness. Where was the Baron? Had he been devoured by the wolf? Mauled by the poodles?

"Oh, *no!*" Quentin swore. "Look!"

Prim and Prude's silhouettes loomed on the crest of the hill.

"They must have heard the dogs barking," Ollie whispered.

The old ladies just stood there for a minute, completely black except for the silver moonlight pooling in the lenses of their glasses. Then they began down the hill. They didn't run, but they were moving quickly—so quickly that it looked like they were gliding down the hill on ice skates. They weren't hobbling at all. There was something horrible about those two old women advancing smoothly down the hill, faster and faster. Prim wasn't even thumping her umbrella for balance. She was holding it out in front of her.

And then, as the kidnappers neared, Anastasia saw that Prim wasn't carrying the umbrella.

She was holding a shotgun. And Prude had one, too.

"Anastasia!" Prim called. "My dear, you'll catch a cold out here." She smiled. She was close enough now for Anastasia to see each and every metal tooth gleaming in the ancient crone's mouth. The Shadowboys cemented against her in terror.

"You mustn't wander after dark," Prude coaxed. "The

night air is very bad for little moppets. Come inside, like a Nice Little Girl."

"This is all your fault, Prude," Prim hissed. "Leaving your post to yammer nonsense at the Mouse Destroyer!"

"He seemed very interested in *The Handsome Rogue Who Fell in Love with the Older Lady*," Prude said.

"Man-mad," Prim snapped. Then she crooned, "Anastasia, come home, dear. We'll make you a nice cup of warm milk." Her head swiveled toward the topiary where the Beastly Dreadfuls crouched. She raised her shotgun and cocked it.

"Awoooooooo!"

The sisters spun around.

"Primrose!" Prude shrilled. *"It's one of them!"*

The wolf vaulted a hedge, green eyes blazing. *"Awoooooooo!"*

Buckshot thundered from the guns. "Smite the wolf! Smite the wolf!"

The wolf crashed from bush to bush, dodging the glittering silver slugs.

"Kill it! Kill it! KILL IT!" Prude screamed.

The wolf let out an *AWOOOOOOOO* of pain.

Anger sizzled Anastasia from her hair follicles all the way to her toenails. She couldn't just stand there and watch as the murderous sisters whacked another trophy to bolt to their dining room wall! The wolf had, after all, saved her from the poodles. Besides, she was an aspiring detective-veterinarian-artist, and the welfare of animals—whether stripy cat or slimy worm—was her concern, even in the midst of a Daring Escape from dastardly kidnappers.

She plunged her hand into her satchel and fumbled through the mice until her fingers closed over her collection of marbles, and then she flung them toward the child-snatchers. Dozens of glass eyeballs twirled across the frosted ground and beneath the old ladies' sensible shoes.

"*Eeeeek!*" cried Prim.

"*Oooooooh!*" hollered Prude.

They slipped and slid on those marbles, their arms flailing in a crazy kidnapper tap dance. They fox-trotted and hula-hustled and do-si-doed and then executed two wild *grands jetés* (that is, sprawl-legged leaps) right into the hole Quentin had been digging for the past week. Their caterwauls rang from the bottom.

"Give me a boost, Prudence!"

Prim's knobbly fingers clawed at the lip of the grave, and then her trampled hat appeared, and her frazzled pink curls, and her glinting glasses, and her fierce teeth.

"We have to run," Quentin urged.

Anastasia nodded, but she also knew that she couldn't lug the snoring mice with her anymore. They were too heavy. At the same time, she couldn't very well abandon them.

Another brainstorm zapped her cranium. She grabbed

the little bottle of smelling salts dangling from the chain at her waist. She uncorked it and opened her satchel and waved it beneath the twitching pink noses of the mice. The mice jolted, their furry eyelids snapping up. They stared at her and then swiveled their heads in unison toward Prim, who was tottering at the edge of the grave, yanking Prude's wrists.

As if moved by a single brain, the mice stormed toward the kidnappers, leaping onto their coats, scurrying up their necks to bite at their faces. The potent smelling salts must have zinged the sensitive mouse-nostrils of even the rodents sleeping in Anastasia's pockets, for her coat began to twitch and shudder as all the mice started elbowing each other to get out, swarming to join their allies in the wild battle.

Prude tumbled back into the hollow, and Prim's gun blasted as she squalled and swung around, mice clinging to her earlobes by their teeth. Skating on the slippery frost, she shot once more before pitching backward into the hole.

"Come on!" Anastasia leapt to her feet and catapulted toward the fence, the Shadowboys scudding alongside her. She reached into her pocket and pressed the button on the electric gate opener. The bars buzzed into action, and the gates slowly butterflied toward the black trees of the Dread Woods.

"Look!" Prude whooped. "There! She's running! And the gates are open!"

"She mustn't get away!" Prim shrieked.

Anastasia's gaze boomeranged to the kidnappers. The old ladies were out of the grave again, and buckshot whizzed and singed the night air in the great battle of wolf and mice versus Watchers. Prude was holding off the animal offensive, and Prim was chasing after the Beastly Dreadfuls. The old woman had thrown down her gun and was racing over the frosty ground and laughing. Her laughter was high and hysterical and evil. Anastasia turned her face back toward the spiked fence and the deep, dark woods that lay beyond it. The Shadowboys had already torpedoed through the open gates, but Prim was going to catch Anastasia— unless . . .

She squeezed the button on the remote control once more. The gates began to swing shut. Anastasia's galoshes thumped. She could hear the electricity humming in the iron bars. Prim was so close behind her that she could smell the sickly scent of her rose-water perfume. There was only a small gap left between the two doors. The thornbushes tore at Anastasia's coat and hair as she burst past them and leapt through the gates at the very last second. The bars clunked shut behind her, with Prim trapped on the other side. Anastasia cried out as the old woman's arm snaked between the bars to grab her braid.

"Little beast!" The words hissed between the silver teeth. Anastasia gasped as the old woman yanked her by the plait until her nose was just inches away from the electrified bars.

"Let her go!" Ollie yelled. "I'll bite you! I'll bite you!"

CRUNCH! Clank! *"Owww!"* Ollie collapsed into a ghostly puddle.

"What did you do to him, you crazy old hag?" Quentin cried.

Prim smiled horribly and raised her other arm. Her knitting needle glinted in her fist, and her furry sleeve rolled back to reveal a row of bracelets stacked on her arm like a silver shell. "It serves you right, you nasty little boy," she spat at the whimpering shadow. "Next time, *I'll* bite *you.*" She gnashed her silver teeth and swiveled her glare back to Anastasia. "So you thought you could get away, did you? Oh, no, my dear dreadful girl. You're not getting away tonight, or any night, for that matter." And the spike arced down toward Anastasia's pitter-pattering heart.

"No!" Anastasia grabbed Prim's wrist. The pointed tip of the knitting needle twinkled just inches from its target. The kidnapper and Anastasia struggled there, panting and desperate as snowflakes sizzled against their sweaty cheeks. The fence buzzed between them. If either Anastasia or Prim even touched one of the bars, they would both be frizzled. Anastasia stared up into Prim's eyes, hypnotized by the hatred burning there. The hungry needle trembled ever closer. The point pressed against Anastasia's chest.

She gulped a tonsil-rattling breath—the type of breath you inhale right before you blow out all the candles on your birthday cake—and huffed it out in one frosty cloud, right onto the lenses of Prim's spectacles. The glass bloomed with the delicate whorls and swirls of Anastasia's crystallizing breath, and then each lens made a funny squeaking noise as cracks spidered across them. Prim let out an enraged scream, her fingers loosening, and Anastasia twisted out of her grasp. The ancient kidnapper lurched, stabbing wildly at the air. But instead of burying itself in Anastasia McCrumpet's almost-eleven-year-old heart, the silver needle clanged against the authentic Victorian fence.

As you may know, silver is an excellent conductor of electricity. The energy simmering and buzzing and trembling in the fence jumped into the knitting needle and jolted up Prim's arm and into her body and sent her flying into the air like a wrinkled rag doll, and then down to the ground perhaps fifteen feet away. Anastasia stared at her. Prim's hat had rocketed off her head and her pink hair was sticking straight out from her scalp. The needle lay beside her scorched hand.

"Victory," Ollie croaked.

Anastasia dashed to his side. "Ollie, are you okay? Did she stab you?"

"No," he mumbled. "I just chomped her silver bracelets. Owwwww. I have a *terrible* toothache."

"ANASTASI*Aaaoooooooo!*"

She whirled. The wolf was galloping toward the fence,

with Prude and the mice swarming behind. Before Anastasia could even twitch a muscle, the wolf hurdled over the iron spikes, clawing the frosty ground as it crashed to a landing beside her.

"Anastasi*oooo*!" it said. "Come with me!"

The wolf was looking right at her, and *it was speaking*. "Get on my *baooowck*! They'll kill us both!"

Had she gone barmy with terror? Wolves didn't speak English! Or Chinese, or Swahili, or Spanish, or any human language, for that matter!

"Hurry!" the wolf shouted. "Get on my back! We *haooooowve* to get out of here!"

As absurd as it all was—as much as she felt she was in a senseless, horrible dream, and as ridiculous as it seemed to climb onto the back of a gigantic talking wolf—this is exactly what Anastasia did. One couldn't exactly say no to a gigantic talking wolf, you understand. She felt the cold swoosh of Quentin and Ollie sliding up behind her onto the wolf's rump.

"Hang *owwwwwwn*!" the wolf bellowed above the din of gunshots and whizzing pellets and squeaking mice. "Hang on and don't let *gawooo*!"

Anastasia wrapped her arms around the wolf's shaggy neck. She took one last look at Prim and Prude and the Baron's brave army of mice and the dark asylum as the

wolf cannonballed toward the trees. If Anastasia had been capable of thinking at that point, she might have wondered whether the wolf was taking her into the forest to eat her. But her mind was a confused jumble of sounds and smells and fear as they smashed through the branches and over the bracken, into a gloom so dark even the blazing full moon couldn't touch it. She buried her face in the wolf's fur. The beast's pulse throbbed in its neck and juddered her arms. They tore deeper and deeper into the Dread Woods. Finally the wolf slowed to an easy lope. Anastasia dared to lift her nose and open her eyes. Her heart still battered against her ribs, but she was suddenly unafraid. She sat up a little on the wolf, the air whooshing through her hair. It was a thrilling, fabulous feeling. It was better than the best bicycle ride you can imagine. And she was alive!

Long, glowing shapes danced ahead. It was the moon shining between trees. The wolf stopped altogether. His sides heaved. He sat down, and Anastasia slid from his shaggy flanks to the frozen earth, the Shadowboys clinging to her.

The wolf turned around and looked at her. His tongue lolled.

"My gosh," he panted. "You're heavier than you look."

Of course, the Shadowboys had hitched a ride on the wolf's back, too, but Anastasia wasn't about to mention that.

Ollie and Quentin slinked into the shadows, hidden and mum.

"Your ear is . . . is bleeding," Anastasia finally stammered, getting to her feet.

"They got some buckshot in my hind end, *tooaoooo*," the wolf sighed. "Bosphorus! This means another trip to the doctor. I'm sure those *owwwwooold* nasties were using silver buckshot."

"Silver buckshot?" Anastasia echoed. "You mean, silver bullets? The kind that's supposed to kill werewolves?" She took a step backward, the fizzy thrill of escape draining away like soda through a sieve. Quentin's shadow arm looped protectively around her shoulders, sending chills down her back.

"Werewolves!" the wolf chortled. He grinned at her. It was a very toothy grin. "There's *noaoooo* such thing as werewolves."

"Oh." Anastasia eyed him. "I thought the Creature in the Woods might be a werewolf. Wait—are you the Creature in the Woods?" she demanded.

"What?" The wolf blinked. "What in blazes are you talking *abowwwt*? What *creature*?"

"The Creature," Anastasia said, "that Prude and Prim are so scared of. They have the fence and those poodles to keep the Creature out, and they're always watching the woods from their tower because they're so frightened. I think

they were even going to . . . feed my heart to the Creature."
She remembered Prude tittering about little bones, and she
shivered as a twig snapped beneath her foot. "Are you *sure*
you aren't the Creature?"

The wolf let out a yodel of laughter. "The Creature in
the Woods!" he said. "By gum, that's a *goowwwood* one." He
shook his bearded head. "These woods are safe and sound.
Just fireflies and squirrels and *owwwwoools*. And the trees
are full of delicious sap for making the Happy Forest Maple
Syrup you drizzle on your *waaoooowffles*."

"No," Anastasia insisted. "I heard them talking about it.
Prude—or was it Prim?—said the Creature made her skin
crawl. They said it could attack at any moment." She took
another step back.

The wolf grinned again. "My dear girl," he said, and it
occurred to her that he was rather a well-spoken wolf, "the
fence and dogs weren't to keep anyone *ooowwooowwt* of the
asylum. All of those precautions were to keep *yawwoooo* in."

Anastasia goggled at him.

"Anastasia," he said softly, "*you're* the Creature."

❈ 27 ❈

Weirder and Weirder

A CLOUD SLIPPED over the moon and plunged the woods into darkness. The wolf's eyes, jolly and clear and green, twinkled at Anastasia. Then, like two Christmas lights flipped off by a switch, they disappeared. The nearby bushes rustled.

"Wolf!" Anastasia cried. "Wolf! Don't go away!"

The moon struggled from the cloud, dappling the forest floor with shimmering light. A large moonlit figure towered beside her. Anastasia jumped as though someone had stuck a pin into her arm.

"Baron!"

He looked puzzled. "Did you whump your head on a tree branch or something?"

"Where *were* you? I thought you were dead as a

dormouse!" To her great embarrassment, tears flooded her eyes and started to drip down her cheeks. "I mean, I didn't see you at all after you went off with Prude. And when the kidnappers came after us . . ."

"Oh, golly. I'm sorry, Anastasia," the Baron said. "You see, I've battled so many child-snatchers in the past, it becomes rather routine. Not that things didn't get a little hairy back there, but . . . I've been through much worse. Of course, you haven't seen anything like that before. You must be scared out of your wits, poor child." He flung back his scarf and reached into the pocket of his bomber jacket—*when had he changed clothes?*—and pulled out a flask. "Have a drink of this," he said. "It will calm you down."

In movies, people usually swill brandy to soothe their nerves after a shock. The Baron's flask, however, contained nothing stronger than ginger ale. Anastasia gulped it down, the bubbles buzzy in her nostrils. She handed the flask back to him. She *did* feel a bit better. "But you still haven't answered my question," she pointed out. "And that wolf . . . Where did that wolf go? Did you see it? It *talked*! That wolf *talked* to me!"

The Baron blinked at her. "Why!" he exclaimed. "I assumed you knew!"

"Knew what?"

"Well, well!" He stroked his mustache. "My dear, that was *me*! I'm the wolf!" His green eyes gleamed at her. "Or rather, I *was* the wolf. I can change back and forth.

Sometimes it's a bit difficult, but on a night like this"—his gaze flicked up toward the moon-tinseled treetops—"it's very easy. In fact, on full-moon nights I usually prefer to go about as a wolf. But it's rather difficult *talking* as a wolf—all teeth and tongue and my vowels come out in yodels—so I'd better stay in man-form now."

"So you *are* a werewolf!" Anastasia exclaimed.

The Baron shook his head, winced, and touched his ear. "Bosphorus, that smarts! No, Anastasia, I told you—there's no such thing as werewolves."

Anastasia also shook her head. The night was getting weirder and weirder. "What did you mean when you said *I'm the Creature*? What creature? Why would Prim and Prude be scared of *me*?"

"Anastasia!" An anxious voice rang out behind them.

Anastasia spun around. "Miss Apple!"

Quentin slithered to the ground as the Mooselick Elementary librarian hurried from between two trees. She knelt to inspect Anastasia's face and ears and pushed the sleeves of her coat up around her elbows, scrutinizing her hands and arms. "Lots of scratches. Not as bad as it could be, though." She hugged her close. "Are you all right? Did those kidnappers hurt you?"

"They made me eat Mystery Lumps. I had to clean a bunch of gross stuff." The words jumbled out. "They locked me up every night and I had to use a chamber pot."

"Despicable!" Miss Apple seethed.

"And they hate mice," Anastasia said. "They're horrible mouse-haters."

"Oh, I know they are," Miss Apple said with a small grin. She hugged Anastasia again.

"Are you okay, Penny?" the Baron asked. "Nobody stepped on you? Squished you?"

"*Squished* you?" Anastasia said.

Miss Apple let out a nervous little laugh. "I'm fine."

"Are you sleepy?" the Baron teased.

Miss Apple let go of Anastasia. Her little librarian's face was bright pink. "Not anymore," she said. "I'm sorry about that, but you know how it is."

The Baron chortled. "Quite all right, sister."

"*Sister?*" Anastasia blurted. "You two are brother and sister?"

"Indeed we are," the Baron said, nabbing Miss Apple in the crook of his elbow and ruffling her hair with his knuckles.

"Stop that!" Miss Apple groused, untangling herself from the Baron's manly noogie. She frowned at him. "Did those kidnappers silver you?"

"I got nicked on my ear," he replied. "And I've got buck-shot lodged in other, more private places."

Miss Apple groaned. "The gluteus maximus again?"

The Baron crimsoned. "Again."

"Miss Apple," Anastasia said, "what in the world is going on?"

Miss Apple nodded. "An excellent question. And I will do my best to answer it to the fullest, but right now the clock is ticking. We must get out of here. Those bounty hunters can't be too far behind."

"Bounty hunters?"

"Kidnappers. Bounty hunters. They've probably called for backup by now," the Baron said. "Those two are in for a world of guano from their bosses. They're going to be desperate to track us down. They'll assemble an angry mob armed with pitchforks and torches and crossbows and guns and knitting needles. They'll burn down this whole forest if they have to, delicious syrup or not, and follow us to the ends of the scorched earth."

Anastasia squeaked.

"By the way, Penny," the Baron said, "did you bring any snickerdoodle cookies? You know those are my favorite escape cookies."

"Snickerdoodle!" Ollie cried. "Oh, I *love* snickerdoodles!"

"Quiet, you pudding!" Quentin hushed him.

The Baron and Miss Apple froze.

"Who said that?" Miss Apple demanded. She peered at the carpet of frosted leaves and pinecones. "Why—! There are two *Shadowboys* here!"

The Baron followed her gaze. "By the marble buttocks of David, so there are!"

Anastasia was flummoxed. Miss Apple and the Baron knew about Shadowboys?

"What are you doing in these woods, children?" Miss Apple asked. "Don't you know about the nasty child-snatchers living nearby?"

"Of course we know," Quentin replied. "We just escaped from them, along with Anastasia."

"They kidnapped us ages ago," Ollie added.

"My goodness!" Miss Apple said. "Well, you can't stay here. You'll have to come with us."

"Thank you," Quentin said, "but we live just a ten-minute Shadowflight away, in Melancholy Falls, and I'm sure our parents are worried about us." He rustled against a tree. "Goodbye, Anastasia. We'll meet again."

"Will we?" Anastasia faltered. "What about your address? And telephone number?"

"I think we'll probably leave Melancholy Falls pretty soon," Ollie said. "The kidnappers knew about us living there, remember."

"Where are *you* going?" Quentin asked Miss Apple.

"Nowhere special," the librarian replied.

Quentin nodded. "Then we'll see you there."

"Oh, but I am sad to say goodbye for now, Anastasia!"

Ollie squeezed her in a cold hug. "I'd change back to boy-form, but I'm wearing my birthday suit," he apologized.

"Goodbye," Quentin said, also giving her a shivery embrace. "We'll see you before long, I promise."

"You can keep my music box until we meet again," Ollie said. "Goodbye, Anastasia! Goodbye!"

And then they melted off into the shadows.

"Goodbye," Anastasia quavered, her chest tightening. Ollie and Quentin were her very best friends in the world. And now they were gone.

"Let's get going," Miss Apple said.

"But, Miss Apple—"

"We'll answer your questions on the way. Come along!" She was now using her no-nonsense Librarian Voice, and the Baron and Anastasia meekly followed her through a tangle of bushes to a moon-spangled glade.

"Ah," the Baron said, his tone warm with admiration. "Here it is."

Anastasia's jaw dropped. "A hot-air balloon!"

"Have you ever flown in one of these?" the Baron asked.

"No," she said. "I've seen them at the Mooselick County Fair, though." The balloon pilot at the fair had waved a gold-topped cane and shouted, "See the world from the perspective of a pigeon or an angel! The Ferris wheel will look like a Tinkertoy to you. Only fifty dollars for the ride of your life!" But Anastasia had not had fifty dollars. She only had enough money to buy a pound of sour watermelon taffy, and she had sadly chewed it while watching Johnny Johnstone, the school bully, float higher and higher and higher, until he was so far away she could no longer hear his snickering. And then she had vomited every bit of the candy back up in front of the dismayed Mooselick County Fairgoers, and that, dear Reader, is the reason Anastasia loathed sour watermelon taffy from the depths of her soul.

"Anastasia," Miss Apple said. "Come along." She scaled a little ladder dangling over the edge of the basket and hopped inside.

Anastasia blinked away her memories. Unlike the bright razzle-dazzle balloons at the Mooselick County Fair, this balloon was a deep, inky, almost-black blue. The wicker basket was blue-black, and the silk balloon puffed above it like a patch of darkest midnight, winking with hundreds of starry little twinkles.

"It's a chameleonic balloon," the Baron whispered. "The pinnacle of balloon technology! Perfect for daring dirigible exploits! It changes to blend in with its surroundings, you see. We'll be invisible to any sky-snooping Watcher!"

"Except for the flames," Miss Apple said. She fussed with a gadget in the middle of the basket, and flames roared from a metallic funnel. "That will get the air nice and hot," she called over the noise. "Hot air rises, you know."

"Once we're in the wild blue yonder," the Baron said, "we'll just look like a star to anyone down below."

Anastasia wondered exactly how high the balloon would take them. It sounded like it was going to be mighty high indeed.

The Baron clapped his hands. "All aboard the H.M.B. *Flying Fox!*"

Anastasia shifted her satchel and scampered up the ladder, slinging her leg over the edge of the basket and tumbling down inside it. Flames sparked at the mouth of the silk balloon, roaring so loudly that Anastasia couldn't hear anything else. She staggered to her feet and watched as the Baron went around untying the ropes anchoring the balloon. There were six ropes, and each one was tied to a little metal stake driven into the ground.

"Ready?" the Baron called, hunkered by the last stake.

Fear and excitement welled in Anastasia's throat. Miss Apple checked a dial on the burner and called, "All systems go."

The Baron undid the knot.

The curious thing about a hot-air balloon is that, even though it zooms upward like a bubble rocketing to the top of a bottle of carbonated soda, it doesn't *feel* like it moves at all. That's how smooth a hot-air balloon ride is. Anastasia watched in astonishment as the moon-blanched forest shrank below them. In the distance she could see St. Agony's Asylum, tiny and far away, as though she were gazing at it through the wrong end of a telescope. She screamed above the roar of the flames, "We're leaving without him! Miss Apple, the Baron's still down there!"

"Actually, his name is Baldwin, dear. He just made up that silly pseudonym to fool those kidnappers," Miss Apple said, still fiddling with the dials. "And he'll be up in a jiffy."

Anastasia turned around just in time to see ten pink fingertips grasping the edge of the basket, and then a tumble of manliness as Baldwin somersaulted inside. "Blooming tulips, I'm out of shape! I used to be a top-notch rope climber." He took out his flask and guzzled from it, and then he reeled all the tethers into the basket.

"Anastasia," Miss Apple said, "look how high we are."

The forest and the asylum were just little dots; then everything was blotted out by mist; then the balloon was actually above the clouds, which billowed beneath them like a silver sea. Miss Apple turned a dial, and the flames snuffed out. The sky was silent and sublime.

"Beautiful," Anastasia breathed. And then she leaned over the edge of the basket and vomited right into the lovely tapestry of glimmering clouds.

"Balloon sickness," Miss Apple said, handing her a crinkling paper sack. Embossed on the side in fancy blue letters were the words OFFICIAL VOMITUS RECEPTACLE OF HER MAJESTY'S BALLOON THE FLYING FOX.

"Don't feel a bit embarrassed," Baldwin reassured her. "Happens to the best of us! I once soiled my best ascot. Have you ever tried to get vomit out of an ascot? Nothing worked. Not soda. Not dry cleaning. I finally had to give up and throw it away. Pity."

Anastasia slid to the floor of the basket, clutching her stomach.

"It will pass, my dear," Miss Apple murmured, crouching beside her and stroking her forehead. "Maybe some ginger ale will settle your tummy. And when you're feeling better, I have sandwiches and cookies."

"Snickerdoodle?" Baldwin asked again.

"I have all kinds of things in the picnic basket," Miss Apple said. "We have a big trip ahead of us."

Anastasia perked up. "How long will it take us to get to Mooselick?"

Miss Apple exchanged a pained look with Baldwin. "My darling," she said, "we're not going back to Mooselick."

"But what about my parents?" Anastasia asked. "Were they really in an accident? Wasn't that just a story Prim and Prude cooked up to trick me into their station wagon? Mom and Dad aren't really"—her voice snagged—"dead, are they?"

Her hopeful gaze double-Dutched between Baldwin and the librarian.

Miss Apple sighed. "You're right, dear. There was no vacuum accident. But both your parents are— Well, they're gone."

"What do you mean, *gone*?" Anastasia cried.

"Your dad is missing," Baldwin said. "We don't know where he is."

"He vanished the same day you were kidnapped," Miss Apple said.

"He's probably looking for me!" Anastasia said. "We have to go to Mooselick! I have to find him!"

"Anastasia." Baldwin pulled a handkerchief from the sleeve of his jacket, covered his nose, and blew it with a mournful honk. "We can't go back. Not for a long, long while. It's far too dangerous. Those kidnappers are going to be looking for you."

Anastasia's shoulders sagged. "What about my mom? Is she missing, too?"

"Oh, d-dear," Miss Apple stammered. "I'm afraid . . . oh, my. Well, child, the thing is—"

"She ran off with a podiatrist!" Baldwin said.

"A—a foot doctor?" Anastasia gasped. "My mother ran away with a *foot doctor*?"

"Yes indeed," Baldwin said. "Dr. Lovelady. He's known"—he lowered his voice—"for being a bit of a quack. Doesn't know a hammertoe from an ingrown nail."

"But apparently he is *very* handsome," Miss Apple said sadly.

"Movie-star looks," Baldwin agreed. "Podiatrists are, in general, the most dashing of all doctors."

"I'm so sorry, Anastasia," Miss Apple said. "After you and your father disappeared, Mrs. McCrumpet packed up and left town. She left no forwarding address."

"But we suspect," Baldwin said somberly, "that they headed to Belgium."

"Why?" Anastasia whispered.

"For the Belgian waffles," Baldwin said. "Naturally."

Anastasia blinked. "Mom didn't even wait to see if Dad and I would come home?"

Miss Apple shook her head. "I'm afraid not. But things aren't exactly what they seem, child. Oh, we have so many strange things to tell you. I suppose this will be the first, and it may come as a shock. So brace yourself, my dear."

Anastasia wiped her nose on her furry sleeve. "All right," she said quietly. "I'm ready."

"Trixie McCrumpet, the lady with whom you have lived for nearly eleven years," Miss Apple said, "is not really your mother."

28
Stars

"SHE IS YOUR stepmother," Miss Apple said.

And the librarian explained that Anastasia's real mother had died nearly eleven years earlier, just a few days after Anastasia was born. "Your father was inconsolable," said Miss Apple. "He went a bit crazy."

"Dilly as a pickle," Baldwin said, tracing a little circle on his temple with his forefinger.

Miss Apple nodded unhappily. "That's when his obsession with vacuums began."

"And he married Trixie Bitterbottom," Baldwin said. "Terrible mistake. Horrible woman."

"Baldwin!" Miss Apple reproached. "Be polite. Anastasia grew up with the woman, after all."

"Your father thought you needed a mother," Baldwin

said to Anastasia. "He thought Trixie Bitterbottom could take care of you. Gosh, was he ever wrong. Trixie couldn't take care of a pet rock."

Anastasia frowned. "She ordered a pet rock off the home shopping channel," she mused. "And one of the googly eyes *did* fall off."

Miss Apple sighed. "I'm sure you love Trixie very much," she said. "I hope this news isn't too upsetting for you."

But surprisingly, it wasn't. Anastasia stared at the sizzling stars and scoured herself for even a molecule of shock. She realized that she had never really *thought* much about Mrs. McCrumpet. Remember, all Mrs. McCrumpet liked to do was to lie in bed and boss Mr. McCrumpet and Anastasia around. She was not a particularly lovable figure. She had never taken Anastasia to the park, or read her a story, or kissed her good night, or sprinkled cinnamon on her toast, or done any of the thousands of motherly things that mothers do for their little ones.

In all the weeks at St. Agony's Asylum, Anastasia had not missed Mrs. McCrumpet once. Just like the uncle that guffaws at his own unfunny jokes or the tattletale cousin or the bristly-chinned grandmother, Mrs. McCrumpet had been, to Anastasia, someone to tolerate. Barely.

Nonetheless, it was rather sad to think that she was, for all purposes, completely alone in the world. Fatherless, stepmotherless, guinea-pig-less . . . she didn't even have two diabolical, child-snatching aunties. What had her mother— her *real* mother—been like? Had Anastasia inherited her freckles and tragic flatulence from her?

And where was Fred McCrumpet? Was he combing Mooselick County for his missing daughter? Or was his disappearance something altogether more sinister?

Anastasia slumped in the basket's wicker belly, wrapped her arms around her legs, and pressed her face against her knees to keep tears from spilling out of her eyes. The balloon was silent for a few minutes.

Miss Apple finally spoke, plucking a leaf from one of Anastasia's bedraggled braids. "My dear, I must thank you for saving my life down there."

"Mine too," Baldwin said. "That was quick thinking with those marbles."

"Saving *your* life, Miss Apple?" Anastasia lifted her chin. "How could I have saved *your* life?"

Miss Apple fumbled with her glasses. "Picking me up and putting me into your pockets when I was—er—incapacitated."

Anastasia stared at her.

"Incapacitated?" Baldwin snickered. "Cheese drunk, I should say!"

"I told you already, I'm sorry about that." Miss Apple looked ashamed.

"Wait," Anastasia said. "Are you saying that *you* ate the cheese, Miss Apple?" She hesitated, thinking of Baldwin gallivanting through the garden as a wolf. "Were you . . . one of the mice?" She felt silly even saying it.

"Not just one of them," Miss Apple answered. "All of them."

"It's a rare talent," Baldwin said. "Hardly anyone can Swarm, but Penny has a real gift for it."

"The problem," Miss Apple said, "is that when your mind is divided into so many different animals, running in all different directions, somersaulting and cartwheeling and running up old ladies' skirts, you don't think very clearly. You don't understand everything that's going on, and your judgment is pretty bad. That's why I couldn't resist that cheese, even though I knew you had painted it with Dr. Bluster's Patented Sleep Preparation. I just *had* to eat it. It was mob mentality."

"Mouse mob mentality," Baldwin added.

"Anyway, Anastasia, I realize that you must have picked up all the mice-me and carried me outside," Miss Apple went on. "That was a wonderful thing to do. Goodness only knows how long I might have lain on the floor of the asylum—and what those mouse-hating women would have done with me." She squeezed Anastasia's shoulder.

"So *you* were all those mice jumping around on the table and biting Prim and Prude?" Anastasia asked.

"Indeed I was," Miss Apple said.

"And you were the mouse that fell onto Prim's hat?"

"Yes." Miss Apple smiled a tiny smile. "But I didn't exactly fall. I leapt."

Anastasia mulled this over. "Well," she said, "that was pretty brave of you. You could have been squished. Prim and Prude went after you with forks and umbrellas. And *you!*" she said to Baldwin. "You fought off the poodles, even though you're poodlephobic!"

"Poodlephobic?" Baldwin's eyes twitched toward Miss Apple. "Nonsense, child. Whatever gave you that idea? Poodles? Ha! I laugh in the face of poodles."

"It didn't matter." Miss Apple's face got very serious. "We had to get you out of there, no matter the risk of—er—squishery. Or poodles."

"We had to help you escape from the clutches of those kidnappers," Baldwin added.

"Who exactly are the Watchers?" Anastasia asked. "I know they kidnap children. They've probably kidnapped hundreds of them. And," she said, "Miss Sneed is a member. She has the eyeball pinkie ring, and her portrait is hanging in the asylum."

"Straight As!" Miss Apple said. "Miss Sneed infiltrated Mooselick Elementary School under the guise of an unlovely secretary, but she was really there as part of Prim and Prude's kidnapping schemes. Unfortunately, we didn't realize that until the morning you were whisked away!"

"But *why* do Prim and Prude snatch children?" Anastasia asked. "I used to think it was to feed the Creature in the Woods . . . but now I know there isn't any creature."

Miss Apple's mouth tightened. "They're part of a ring called CRUD. It's an entire committee of kidnappers—they call themselves Watchers—trained to grab children deemed . . . potentially dangerous. And if they confirm their suspicions—well, the children come to a very bad end."

"CRUD stands for *Committee for Rubbing-out Unnatural Dreadfuls*," Baldwin said.

"Potentially dangerous?" Anastasia echoed. "Unnatural dreadfuls?"

She flashed back to the ominous words scrawled on Lucy Pinkerton's photograph: TO THE DREADFUL. How had little pigtailed Lucy been dreadful and dangerous? For that matter, how could *Anastasia* possibly present a threat to anyone? It made sense that Prim and Prude snatched Quentin and Ollie. Shadowbites were deadly. But she, Anastasia, was just a freckled almost-eleven-year-old who dinged a triangle in the Mooselick Elementary School band.

"Why would they think *I* might be dangerous?" she asked.

"Oh, they thought you might be dangerous, all right," Baldwin said. "That's why Primrose and Prudence were so afraid of you. That's why they locked you up every night at sundown."

Anastasia's mind carouseled with memories of her awful days at the asylum. The long nights trapped in Room Eleven. The way Prim and Prude watched her out of the corners of their eyes. The strange conversations she had overheard.

"But," she said, "they were always watching the woods, like they were afraid of something that might live there."

"I imagine they *pretended* to be afraid of the woods," Baldwin said, "to make *you* afraid of them. That way, you'd be less likely to run away."

"And they were being careful kidnappers," Miss Apple said. "They were keeping a lookout for anyone who might come to rescue you."

"That's why we had to orchestrate a mouse invasion," Baldwin said. "So that when I arrived on their doorstep as a capable mouse exterminator, Prim and Prude wouldn't just throw me out on my nose. They were so desperate to get rid of the mice, and so afraid that someone from the Health Department might come and discover *you*, that they *invited me inside*. They pretty much had to. A brilliant plan, really."

"We're just sorry it took us so long to get there!" Miss Apple cried. "You had to live with those nefarious agents of CRUD for far too long! Well over a month!"

"We had to find you," Baldwin said, dabbing his eyes.

"And then we had to figure out how to gain entry to the asylum. But Penny's ever so right." He made a sad little yodeling noise into the hankie. "You could have met with a terrible fate."

"Don't apologize," Anastasia said hastily. "I'm just glad you came at all. I mean, why did my—er—*fate* matter so much to you? I know that you're a super librarian, Miss Apple, but I didn't think that librarians went after child-snatchers and that sort of thing."

"Oh, Anastasia!" Miss Apple said. "Of course your fate matters to us! We care very much! You see, Anastasia . . ." She paused and took a deep breath. "I am your aunt. Your *real* aunt. And Baldwin is your uncle."

"We know this must seem incredible to you," Baldwin said, "particularly after those bosphorus kidnappers pretended to be your great-aunts. Those festering crab apples! Those boorish gobgrinders! Scum of the earth! SCUM—"

"Shhhh!" Miss Apple hushed him in a stern Librarian Voice. She gazed down into Anastasia's freckled face and continued in a softer tone. "Dear, I have watched you grow up. I followed behind the school bus on your very first day of kindergarten, and every single day thereafter. I took that librarian job at Mooselick Elementary to be close to you."

"Really?" Anastasia asked. She thought back to all the pleasant afternoons in the tiny school library, snuggled into one of the tatty beanbag chairs, sipping Miss Apple's hot cocoa and reading Francie Dewdrop mysteries. She remembered how she had always felt at home with the mousy little librarian, and she knew—somewhere in her heart she was certain—that Miss Apple was indeed her aunt, as surprising as the news may have been.

"Really." Miss Apple pulled her into a hug.

"But why didn't you ever tell me?" Anastasia asked.

Miss Apple sighed. "It's a long story, child. You see, your father refused to see anyone from our family, ever since . . . well . . ." Her voice trailed off, and she stood up and fiddled with a gold-plated gadget on the balloon's burner. "It was a complicated situation. There was a big family fight, I'm afraid. Years and years ago. But Fred is our brother."

"And that makes *you* our niece, Anastasia," Baldwin said, his green eyes twinkling at her.

Miss Apple cleared her throat. "Our family," she said in the quietest of quiet Librarian Voices, "is not entirely *ordinary.*"

Anastasia sank into thought. Miss Apple—her *real* auntie—could transform into mice. Uncle Baldwin could change into a wolf. Obviously the McCrumpet family tree flourished with fruit much stranger than she could have ever imagined. Was that why Fred McCrumpet had kept mum about their relatives all these years?

And perhaps she, Anastasia, the littlest apple of all on this peculiar family tree, was not quite the completely average almost-eleven-year-old girl she had always considered herself to be. She liked to eat moths, she reflected. That was a bit odd. But her curious new appetite for fuzzy insects was just the effect of rampant hunger . . . wasn't it? And she *could* frost glass with her breath. However, as interesting as this talent may have been, it didn't seem particularly dangerous.

"Why," she asked again, slowly and thoughtfully, watching her aunt and uncle closely, "did Primrose and Prudence think I could be *dangerous*?"

Miss Apple and Baldwin exchanged another Serious Grown-Up Look.

Then Miss Apple sighed and smiled. "We have so very much to talk about."

"But before we do any of that," Baldwin said, unfolding his long manly legs and standing up, "come look at the stars, Anastasia."

The moon blazed bright as a spotlight, and the stars sizzled like they had never sizzled before. You may have had similar views from the window of an airplane, but they have

never been as clear as the view from a hot-air balloon. The stars seemed as close as candles sputtering on a birthday cake, as though Anastasia's cheeks might get burned if she leaned too far over the edge of the balloon's wicker basket. As though she could huff out the entire Milky Way with one big magical birthday-wish breath. It was so lovely that her almost-eleven-year-old heart swelled.

Did you know that your heart is about as big as your fist? Curl your fingers to your palm, and you will have a good estimate of the size of your heart. Muffy, the guinea pig with anger-management issues, had a grumpy little heart the size of a raspberry. When Miss Apple stormed through the asylum as a mischief of mice, her heart was divided into hundreds of tiny rodent tickers each the size of a garbanzo bean. Within the slick chest of a blue whale throbs a heart weighing one hundred pounds. A blue whale's heart is so large that you could stroll through each of the four chambers, if you were willing to squeeze through the valves.

Anastasia McCrumpet's heart was about the same size as yours. In that moment, however, her heart felt as big as the heart of a blue whale. It was the first night that she had been able to see stars since Primrose and Prudence plucked her from her absolutely ordinary life back in the humble town of Mooselick and forevermore changed her fate. It was the first time that she had not been locked away from their starry and lovely and phosphorescent and effervescent magic. Her heart felt big and full.

Anastasia reached for Miss Apple's hand with her own freckled one, and took Baldwin's in her other.

And the H.M.B. *Flying Fox* sallied forth into the birthday-cake-candle night.

As you will remember, attentive Reader, Miss Viola's Memories book included a Victorian newspaper advertisement praising a guide to nineteenth-century manners. For your edification and improvement, the publishers of this book have kindly reproduced essential points from Miss Drusilla Jellymonk's

Etiquette Manual
for the
Prim and Proper Sort

✻ The Prim and Proper Sort will never acknowledge a guest's foul body odor. You should instead unobtrusively open the window and jump out.

✻ If you notice that your visitor's ears are unclean, do not call attention to their subpar hygiene with a thoughtless comment. Instead, discreetly insert the tip of your umbrella into the offending ear canal(s) and twist gently until all wax has been removed.

✻ In the unlikely but possible event of inviting a zombie to tea, the Prim and Proper Sort endeavors to provide guests with brain and cucumber dainties. Should brain be unavailable, ladyfingers may suffice.

✻ The Prim and Proper Lady never uses her sleeve to wipe crumbs from her upper lip. She extricates food particles with an elegant mustache comb.

✻ When dining out-of-doors with friends, bring a child or two along. Should a ravenous bear interrupt your picnic, politely offer your unexpected guest an urchin upon which to snack, and then return to conversing with your invited company.

Out and About

❧ Should flatulence strike at the symphony, the Prim and Proper Sort synchronizes his or her toots with the brass section. This demonstrates knowledge of music.

❧ While perambulating in the park, you may encounter a friend with her new baby. If said baby is hideous, it is incumbent upon you to refrain from commenting on the infant's appearance. You must therefore pretend not to see the baby. If your friend mentions the baby, look around in a show of confusion and say, "What baby?" Keep up the farce for the duration of your encounter.

❧ If you have stepped in chewing gum, use your handkerchief—*not* your bare fingers—to remove the offending globule from your shoe. Then place the globule into your mouth as discreetly as possible.

❧ When comforting a seasick friend, encourage their swift recovery by mentioning that your fellow passengers are concerned—concerned that the revolting retching emitted by your traveling companion will ruin everyone's teatime. If that doesn't work, spare your friend social disaster by throwing them overboard.

When visiting an insane acquaintance at the lunatic asylum, compliment them on their fetching straitjacket. If your friend lacks this accessory, talk to an administrator and urge the asylum to fit your friend with a straitjacket at once. This is called *consideration for others*.

— Funerals —

When attending a funeral, the Prim and Proper Sort wears black, as dark clothing is slimming and always fashionable. (A note to Prim and Proper Ladies: veils are particularly attractive mourning accoutrements, and useful for hiding your smile.)

If you aren't really sad, then you can hire an orphan to cry on your behalf. Orphans have plenty to cry about.

If you happen to be a skilled taxidermist, offer your services to the grieving family at half price.

Funerals can be terribly dreary. To improve the mood, set up a lighthearted game of tiddlywinks atop the casket.

If you are the bereaved, you will be expected to host a reception after the service. While inconvenient, the purpose of this gathering is to compensate your friends for the extreme displeasure of attending a funeral. Remember: mourners expect salami.

— Criminal Diversions —

Arsenic is best delivered via a teatime treat, sprinkled upon scones, watercress sandwiches, or muffins. Murder after five in the evening would be improper and a mark of bad breeding.

If your criminal pastimes require preparation of a blackmail note, avoid the gauche contemporary fashion for cutting letters from periodicals and pasting them into your message. Nobody enjoys receiving an epistle of doom that is *sloppy*! Strive for elegant penmanship when writing out your blackmail demands, and *do* use high-quality stationery.

— Charitable Endeavors —

The Prim and Proper Sort makes every effort to improve the existence of the world's Downtrodden and Wretched Types.

🦋 Enrich an orphan's life by giving them the opportunity to clean out your top-rate chimney. Few orphans have the good fortune to see the interior of a chimney as fine as yours! If you are feeling especially generous, position a second ragamuffin at your doorway. *Perfect* doorstop.

🦋 Consider adopting a poodle. Poodles are loyal and intelligent creatures and make fine walking companions. And should a gust of wind blow away your wig, the poodle will make an attractive temporary replacement.

That Horrid Thing: Your Body

🦋 It is indelicate to sweat from your armpits. Strive to sweat from your elbows or knees instead.

🦋 Spitting is to be scrupulously avoided, even when you are by yourself. Therefore, you must give up the nasty habit of brushing your teeth.

REGARDING FLATULENCE:
🦋 The Prim and Proper Sort does *not* pass wind. This foul act will ruin you socially. If you let one rip in front of company, expect to be selling matches on the street within the month.

❧ That said, should one of these noxious emissions slip from your bustle or trousers, there are a few desperate measures to which you *must* resort to cover your gaffe.

❧ Burst into an operatic aria.

❧ Muffle the noise by sitting on a small child.

❧ Blame it on someone else.

❧ Faint.

❧ If a man, nod somberly and murmur, "War injury."

❧ Finally, the Prim and Proper Sort does not poop. Ever.

— A Note to — Good Little Boys and Girls

Children should be neither seen *nor* heard. If you happen to be one of these lousy ankle-biters, *please* do the world a favor and lock yourself into a cupboard or trunk until your eighteenth birthday. Study this etiquette manual in the years between now and then. When you finally pass from your filthy grub stage into adulthood, you may then emerge as a Prim and Proper Butterfly, ready to dazzle the world.

* * THE AUTHOR WISHES TO THANK * *

Brianne Johnson
Matchless Lady Agent of Letters
Acclaimed Mesmerist
and
Mistress of the Hula Hoop

&

Shana Corey
Thrice-Crowned Unicycle Championess
Purveyor of Best-Quality Peppermint Tonic
and
Editrix Extraordinaire
(Fine-Tuning Literary Devices and Pianofortes since 1893)

* * * * *in addition to* * * * *
the Marvel-Working Joy-Practitioners at
Random House Children's Books

HOLLY GRANT has loved spine-tinglingly spooky stories since she was your age. If Holly were a kangaroo, she would always keep a good mystery novel in her pouch. If she were a spider monkey, she would climb up to the tippy-top shelf where all the secret books are hidden in the public library. If she were a human, she would have been able to type this story herself, instead of dictating the entire manuscript to a suspiciously monobrowed secretary named Miss Sneed. Visit Holly and the Beastly Dreadfuls at BeastlyDreadfuls.com.

JOSIE PORTILLO was born and raised in Los Angeles, where she works as a freelance illustrator. She draws inspiration from mid-century design, vintage children's animation, and her surroundings (fortunately, she does not live in an authentic Victorian lunatic asylum). When she's not illustrating, she can be found spending time with her two dogs (they are not vicious attack poodles) and playing soccer (though she hears catching leeches is also excellent exercise). She claims she has never met a suspiciously monobrowed secretary named Miss Sneed in her life.